IN THE SHADOW OF THE SPRINGS I SAW

Publication Modjaji Books © 2022
Text Barbara Adair © 2022

www.modjajibooks.co.za

ISBN 978-1-928433-47-7

Supervisor for PhD and editor: David Medalie
Book and cover design: Brenton Maart with Barbara Adair
Text design and typesetting: Brenton Maart

IN THE SHADOW OF THE SPRINGS I SAW

BARBARA ADAIR

Art is anything that you can get away with ...
Take some chocolate
and take 2 pieces of bread,
and then put the chocolate
in the middle of the bread
and you make a sandwich.
That's a cake.

modjaji books

She is dressed in black jeans and a white T-shirt.

Thin. She does not lean against the wall of the building for the white T-shirt will get dirty as the walls of the building are dirty, very dirty. She stands upright, her blue and black leather bag tucked under her arm. She is afraid that should she not hold it firmly it will be taken away by someone who can run faster than she can.

This is 2nd Ave in Springs.

The building on the opposite side of the street reflects in the black lenses of her sunglasses, it is painted white but the white is now off white, the six balconies on the six floors that are visible in the front of the building are painted red, blood red, the blood of dead chickens. Below the second floor red balcony is a fast food outlet; on the first floor, which is the second floor, behind wide glass windows are tables, many people sit at them, she is unable to see what is on the tables but as it is a fast food outlet she knows that it must be the food that they have bought and are now eating. Below this is the entrance to the food outlet. It is also painted red and white. Kentucky Fried Chickens squawk as they are rolled in batter and served with coleslaw and mash potato.

She tastes the tobacco from the rolled up cigarette that the man next to her smokes, it tastes less like battery chicken and more like the natural-ness of Zimbabwe farmlands.

She waits for Mosheen. He owns the building that she stands in front of, and he owns the one opposite her, the building with the red and white balconies. She must wait for Mosheen is busy for he also owns the chemist, Hoppies Chemist, the chemist in the building next to which she stands. And the chemist today is very busy for this is the only chemist in Springs.

Is it possible to speak to the owner of that building, the one over there, the one where the Kentucky Fried Chicken outlet is?

Mosheen, yes you can, he is the owner of this chemist.

Hoppies Chemist has always been Hoppies Chemist. Twenty years ago it was Hoppies Chemist in Springs, a town that was populated by white people. And when black people moved into the town, the chemist was sold by the white people who owned it to Mosheen, they thought he was a fool, it would not do to own a chemist in an area mainly populated by black people for white people know that

black people have their own medicine, they do not go to chemists, they are superstitious and backward. Yes Hoppies Chemist would not be a very profitable business.

Charles is wiry and short, the man to whom she speaks does not have a South African accent.

She speculates, Nigerian? Ghanaian?

Yes, wait, he will come to you, his son is not here today, his son is also a chemist, and so he has a lot of prescriptions to attend to, it is a busy day today. Charles turns towards a young man whose hair is matted and dreadlocked, hold on, you can stand there, no there.

A woman and a child walk towards Charles, the woman holds out a plastic bag, it has the words Hoppies Chemist written in black on it, Charles looks into the bag, he counts its contents, then he looks at the invoice that she hands to him. He waves her forward. A young boy, he looks to be about fifteen, is behind her. He too hands Charles a bag, Charles looks into it and then he checks the invoice. The young boy holds the right hand of an old man, he guides the old man, helps him move his one foot forward, then the other, inch by inch.

Go now you are OK. And you, go, and you, he points at her, you, you can go down there, Mr Mosheen is free now, there go into the office at the back.

There is a plastic jar of Epimax E45 cream on the shelf to her right, citro-soda in a green and white bottle to her left, Aspirin in red and white cardboard boxes on the same shelf, Panado and Grandpa headache powders. As she walks further down, on the shelf in front of her is Benylin cough mixture, then hair dye and hair straightener, Dark and Lovely, and vitamins and Durex condoms.

Hi, good morning, is it possible that we go inside that building, yes that one, the one, the one with the red balconies, where the Kentucky Fried Chicken is? I am told that you own it?

You want to go upstairs, not just into where they have the tables, upstairs, further than the second floor, it is dark there, nothing up there, do you have a torch? I will give you Cyril, he will take you there, you must go through the side passage, the door on the second floor is locked and I don't have access there. Fine, no problem I will call Cyril.

She walks with Cyril into the building that is across the road. The smell of old cooked oil hangs in the air, behind a steel grille are workers, most of them are women, they wear white hair nets on their heads. The women fry chicken and serve chicken and hand chicken to clients and take money and smile.

The best place is the next floor, it has been redecorated, it is clean and workers clean it up all the time because people sit there and eat, come I will show you. You want to go further up? Why? It is just dirty and broken down and dark, no-one goes up there. The Kentucky Fried Chicken people, they rent the whole building, but they don't use it, they just use the ground floor and the first floor, they use some space on the next floor to store things, but they don't need the whole building, they just rent it, they have a lot of money, and a lot of business and I think that they rent the whole building so that people won't move in upstairs, people need to live somewhere and if they did not keep it locked, people would move in. It smells up there, from all the chicken and the dirt, it is not clean, and there are broken toilets and windows. I say that they should renovate it, renovate this building, take out all the old stuff, all these floors, these wooden floors, put in tiles, easy to clean, fix the bathrooms, you can get nice and cheap taps and stuff from the bathroom shop in the Mall, then they could, or my boss could, rent the rooms out. And look here, they must take these windows out, they are such a strange shape, these rooms just need windows that can open wide so that the air can come in. I think that if the Kentucky Fried Chicken people renovated it they could have all their workers living here then they would not have to travel, or otherwise my boss could earn more money. He is rich; he owns the chemist and this building. There are so many people here in town, so many; they need a place to live, and the chemist, it is so busy because it is far to go to the Mall, no-one wants to have a chemist here now, but my boss, he does, and look, it is full.

Hey, Kevil, that is my boss's daughter's husband, he comes from Mauritius, I don't know why he is here the daughter should be living with his family, that is the way it must be done. In my culture, I come from Venda, the woman always goes to live with the man's family. I don't know why he is here. Hey Kevil, hey man.

My boss, he must help people with a place to live but then he can also make money. My place he gives me for free because I work for him, it's on the top floor of the chemist building, I've lived here for fifteen years that's how long I have been working there for him. He is a good guy, ja but he does not want all these people living with him, all these foreign people, and I don't also, but he could fix up here, it would be better. It smells up here, chicken, if the people downstairs could smell this they would not come to this place and buy lunch. Careful, the floors are not even, don't trip up, and look there is a pigeon, it is dead, it is rotting, maybe that is why there is a smell, that bird must have flown in through this window, look the glass is broken, and it could not get out. No, the plumbing is not working up here, only downstairs, they have toilets on the second floor, for the clients you know, but not up here, they don't want to spend money.

No, they are different to us some of the people that have come to Springs, fifteen years ago when I came to work for my boss they were not here like they are today, it's like they are different to us, they don't speak our languages. I don't know who owns the Kentucky Chicken, I think it is a guy from Pakistan, but I don't know. This Pakistani guy buys something that comes from America, and they won't even let Pakistanis go to America, someone told me that they hate them there, they hate the Muslims. My boss he is a Muslim, I don't think I could hate him, I am a Christian, but he has been good to me and my wife. I told you he gives me the room for free, I like the place where I live, it is on the top of the building where the chemist is, but I don't really have friends here, I don't want to invite these people to where I live, they are not like us you know, different, some don't even look like us even though they are black. My child, he is in Grade 4, ten years old, he goes to that school over there, look there, look out of this window, where all those kids are playing, that's his school, and some of them go to the school. When he is done, they stop school at lunch time, I bring him home and make him stay inside, I don't want him to get involved with all the drugs, he must just learn, get education. Today he is inside because the schools are closed, those kids in the field, I don't know who they are, but I keep him away when the teachers are not there, it's better.

You ask me do I feel safe with them all out there. Can I feel OK if they are outside? I don't want anyone to come into my house, but if they don't take my job, if they don't want to marry my children then they are fine. I will not give up my house; I will not give what is mine. I am the man in my house; I am in charge of my house and my wife and my child. I will only feel safe if I keep them under control, they can't take over. I want to close

the doors if I don't want them, if I don't like them.

Careful, these stairs are steep, let me point the light, my phone has a light, put on yours then it will be better, come. Let us go out.

She walks out of the building and turns her head to look at a building that is to her right, a child hangs wet washing on a stretched out rope that is held between two pillars that are at either side of the balcony. Several shirts and some linen are already blowing in the slight wind, orange and blue, flags wave in the wind, flags of surrender or flags of victory? The child stoops under the weight of the wet clothing?

She glances down at a battered book she bought from the Afrikaans bookseller who sets up a table every day at the entrance of Park Station in Johannesburg. She passes his table often as she walks from the station to the university, carefully holding her bag close to her chest. It was only once that she stopped to look at what he had on his table. Many books, religion and self-help, is religion self-help, look inside yourself and you will find your inner god, there is an old book, she cannot make out the date when it was published or who the publishers were, an old book with pictures of old Art Deco buildings in it.

Chapter Heading - Where are these buildings?

In Springs.

The architects and builders dug and poured concrete and laid bricks and painted and made balustrades of wrought iron; they did not think that the floor on which they built was much older than they were. Underneath the concrete floor could be the site of an indigenous gold miner who searched for the skeins of gold that were rumoured to be found here on this land, he created his home on this soil. Underneath this floor, this floor on which the indigenous miner built his home, is a pit. This was where he dug down far into the earth in order to store his bread and meat for below the surface it is cool and he does not want the sun to rot his food. And in this pit there were artefacts, part of a wall, a stone spear, and in the floor were the fossilised remains of cow dung and a flower.

She raises her head and looks at the apartment building that is to her right; the balconies, which are on either side of the six Grecian columns that hold up the name of the building, Court Chambers, have rounded metal railings. The child who was hanging the washing out to dry has now moved off the balcony, only the laundry blows there now, white sails, the ship moves forward. A woman stands on another one of the balconies, she

is higher than where the child was, it must be the on the fourth floor. She beats a red and blue blanket; there is some form of design in its centre, the colours of the Zimbabwean flag. In the windows of the rooms there are shadows, a shadow of a curtain, a shadow of the wronged dead tapping. Several children stand at the entrance to the building. She can hear their voices.

She walks across the road. A man sits on a chair outside the building. His eyes, the eyes of an animal stalking its prey, stare at her.

May I go inside please?

Certainly, come I will unlock the entrance gate, I do not allow anyone in here, but you, all of you, you do not look as if you want to steal, you can go inside.

The windows of the building look inwards and they look outwards, they are both square and round; the round windows are smaller than the square ones. The metal frames are painted red. Children, both small and big, line the metal horizontal rails on which are snake-like designs, the designs crawl and undulate across the small hands. The laundry hangs out to dry, it is many-coloured. The children stare at her and laugh and jump and shout. They are at home today for the schools are closed, it is school holidays. They dance in the open corridors and hang on the railings, the building is built around a central space, she looks down into it, there are garbage bags and a few barely alive pot plants. The metal is red and hot.

This is a home, a picture of a child's mind.

She wonders if the children will remember this home, their home. If they will remember the ghosts that they meet in the stairwells; the ghosts of legend, European legends set in twisting Art Deco curlicues, ornate railings and rounded towers?

A home is the receptacle of memory; a memory of all the things that are forgotten, or that we want to forget, the soul, of you, of me, of the child that poses for the photograph that she takes. Memory invades a home; it is contained in the walls of the rooms that are lived in.

Somewhere someone once said: We can write a room and read a home for a home unlocks the door to daydreaming.

She walks up some stairs; the lifts do not work, a child holds her hand and points to a doorway.

This is my home, he says.

Where are we going to?

Springs, the town on the East Rand.

Do you mean the season?

Ah, the season, Springs, it is a seasonal town.

The town, yes I do know it. I have
been there, but it was a long while
ago, an old gold mining town isn't it.

A dead town.

No, Springs is growth, new growth,
but in Springs it is now autumn.

It is a nothing space, a dead space, a dirty space.

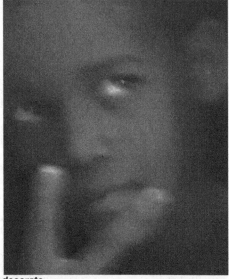

There is a lot of trash in it, but look
between the garbage at the Art Deco
buildings, one of the best western
architectural styles.

Decorations decorate.

Art Deco, the birth of a flower; it was
a movement of ideas, an architecture
of buds; curls, swirls and
new born petals?

Springs, it is a cemetery.

That's autumn, everything is dying.

It is a cemetery this town, yet it is a distorted cemetery for
the graves are filled with life.

The buildings are tombs, structures
that house the dead. Watch the
dead people, watch them move and
dance. They are the waking dead, the
walking dead.

Ah, a dead man coming out of a tomb is the best master of
life for he knows its value.

The window panes are dirty, dust; the
metal work does not shine.

Look, all the buildings face the sun, blue and red
window panes turn towards the sun. There is value
in a ray of light; it is the value of warmth.

There is a beauty in these buildings;
illusion, existence and status; they
all go together, they are not there yet
they exist and live again.

It's a hell hole.

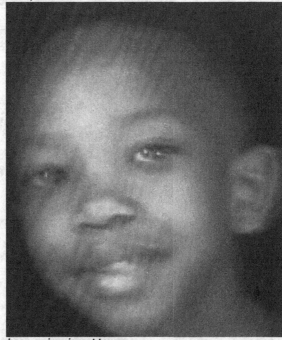

Things will always grow up again; the seeds of the dead are planted in Springs.

The people; Somalis, Ethiopians, and Nigerians, Pakistanis and Bangladeshis, they are the seeds now, their histories; their movement defines this space, they are the flowers that flourish. The Greek, the Portuguese, the Jew, the Italian, they walk the streets, they have no home here anymore, they make but a stain on a wall, indelible, their souls are here now.

Springs is an immigrant town.
It has always been an immigrant town.
We are afraid.
Of whom?
The dirt, it is dirty now.
Of what?
The ghosts, they are everywhere.
Who knew the beauty of the Art Deco architecture?
This is a dead town.
It's a ghost town.
Springs; this place is like somebody's memory of a town.
And the memory is fading.
Ghosts are not real.
We are all ghosts.
Ghosts have no memory.
We have no memory.
We will remember through the spaces that are lived in.
What are we waiting for?
For it to be too late.

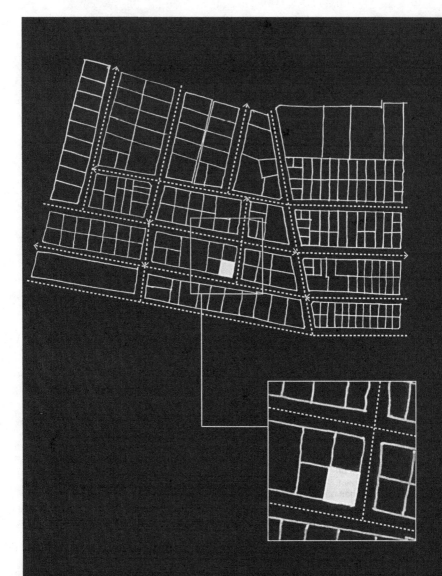

[parabolic vault – a vault that is shaped in the form
of a curve made from concrete]

[undulating – in architectural terms this is the intersection of
convex and concave curves. art deco buildings undulate]

lean candles hunger in
the silence a
brown god
smiles between greentwittering
smoke from broken eyes
a sound
of strangling breasts and bestial
grovelling
hands rasps the purple
dark-
ness
a
prostrate within twitching shadow
lolls
sobbing
with
lust

She stumbles, the paving is uneven

for the cement between the stones is chipped and broken, tough green and brown weeds grow up between the gaps, a gaggle of ants walks a black line into a rotting plastic bag in which the remains of a chicken create an unpleasant perfume that permeates the dust in the air. There is a confusion of brown and yellow, the pavement stone hills are annoying and hazardous if she does not concentrate as to where each foot is placed when she walks and the rotting plastic bags may make her slip. She does not look at the faces of those others who pass by her for she focuses only on where each foot is placed, but when she does look up she watches others with a fixed stare, as if she knows each person at whom she looks, she knows his age, occupation, sexual history, political affiliations, the names of his family and friends, where he comes from and for how long he has been in this town. But she does not know this; she just might if she tries hard enough. For a minute she lifts her head and is mesmerized by the dancing harlequin clothes of a young man, red and white trousers, an orange and blue shirt, his shaven head covered by a black beret that has rainbow badges on it, and then he is returned once more into the crowd at the entrance to Hatties Fashion, the clothing shop in Shimwells building in 2nd Avenue outside of which is a sign that says 'SALE'. She looks at the red pillars that hold up the building, many buildings are red in this town, red, a gay colour, bursting with light, and then she stops and raises her head, the brown elevated writing lifted on the white painted wall above the red pillars says Shimwells, 1933. She leans forward to tie a shoe lace that seems to have come loose, then she stretches up and looks at the road beside her: cars surge, some are old and tired, smoke comes from exhausted exhaust pipes, lorries with flapping olive green canvas grind and scream as they stop at the traffic light, wheels and brakes compete as to which has the greater sound, more cars leap upwards and forwards, a red Ferrari, incongruous and open topped, the driver's sunglasses gleam and his gold watch flashes lightning, motorcycles swerve around deep potholes, a mechanical noise, electric, a choreographed soundtrack made up of the high notes of the violin and the harsh smash of cymbals. She does not continue walking; she seems to need

to rest, she rests her back against the pillar, a small cat with no particular markings except for a red blaze across his left eye darts into a drain, then five minutes later, he creeps out slowly, a whisker appears, a sharp tooth, a diamond gleaming eye. There is order in this chaos; everything dances to a divine beat. She is completely lost, she dreams, and yet she knows where she stands, her vigilance betrays her, she can tell you the names of all the streets and buildings, she holds her bag tightly, her cellular phone held firmly in a hard hand. She is not confused; her progress is a perfectly plotted trajectory through this crumbling urban space. Then there is a face she recognises, or does she? Are his age, his occupation, his sexual history, his political affiliations, the names of his family and friends; are they all just something she can imagine, she sees a stereotype that only she can speak for? There is no need to hear your voice for I can tell your story better than you can speak it yourself, there is no need to hear your voice, just tell me a short story and then I will tell it back to you, tell it back to you so that it is mine. As I write you, I write myself for you are the centre of my speech. And in the second that she stares and writes the story of his life, his age, his occupation, his sexual history, his political affiliations, the names of his family and friends, he walks forward and into the arms of a child who is dressed in a blue and white T-shirt and scuffed shorts that are made of denim. The child does not walk, he stumbles in two twisted rusted iron clad legs.

SMELL THE FLOWERS WHILE YOU CAN

To: B
From: A
Re: Springs

Hey, what a surprise to find the mail from you this morning. Yes I still live on the East Rand, in Springs, and no nothing except the colour of my hair has changed. I am sedentary, don't go out that much, I mainly just sit on my chair, on the balcony, or if it is cold, inside, and look out onto the street. I can look out when I am inside too. It is sometimes dangerous outside, only sometimes though. I watch the movement of the people in the street and in the buildings and shops opposite me. I like to think of change in terms of movement. I give change power? I wonder why? Is it because I do not move? I do not change? Sometimes I do go out, I just go out of my flat and watch, just stand on the corner next to the busy road and imagine that this is the ocean, and I just watch the movement, the waves, the dance, the ballet of the space, the ocean sea. The sea is a mirror, it reflects these streets, faces of people stare only at themselves. The movement of time, time continues, does that sound philosophical? And now that I am thinking philosophically, there is the body, there is the arbitrary rushing of the stars, and of course, you remember what my passion was, dance. Maybe I think of movement and dance as I am unable to dance anymore. Yesterday, it was in the evening and the night was warm, I watched two people, an older man and a young boy. The older man looked like a drug dealer? Am I being presumptuous here, a stereotype? There are a lot of drug dealers in this street. He wore dark glasses and a head band tied across his forehead. On each finger of both his hands he wore a ring. I am sure that I saw the winking of diamonds in those rings. And the young boy, well he was just a boy. The man was teaching the boy to ride a bicycle. He held the boy around his waist so that he remained upright and did not fall over onto the road, it was elegant and lithe. For a long time I watched them move in the moonlight, slowly. The adage is a slow movement performed with fluidity and grace, the movement creates the feeling of ease. The boy and the man performed the adage. I felt happy, I am happy that I have this memory. Where are you, and what are you doing?

You once told me that when something changes there is a change in texture, in texturalness. Change always results in a change in space. The change may be one in which the space becomes more fluid, ice melts and becomes water, there is a smooth movement from one space form to another, from one textual form to another. Sometimes this is best illustrated by something that becomes rotten, change may be compared to the change in a cat, once it dies and is left on a hot pavement, it will putrefy and decay and spread its guts out. There is a texture to a rotting body. There is a texture to the live body. And of course the space of the pavement is also changed; its texturalness is softened, rotting bodies make the asphalt softer. In change there is always a change of nature and so purpose; space changes by a deliberate movement, a walking slowly away, a walking slowly towards.

The dead can walk, although they can't run. And the dead are never textured, just texture.

There is no running in change; there is only a slight expressionless change, minute by minute, second by second, hour by hour. It is no longer the same as it was before this movement, it is changed.

What is Art Deco but a movement of ideas; the buildings are textured in the curving designs, and the outsider moved into the inside from the outside.

Ideas move when the outsider moves in; Jews, Portuguese, Congolese, Christian, Muslim and Pakistani. And the texture of those that walk on the pavement must change the space, changes the buildings, the undulating curves.

What is Art Deco and the stories that surround it?

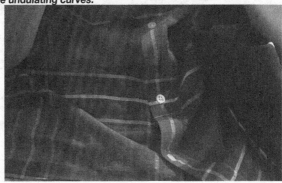

He is not a tall man but he has a tall presence.

He towers above them as he looks up, and he is sitting down. He has black hair and his skin is dark. His eyes too are dark. They stare out of the window, they look beyond her, outside her, outside to the road where the traffic begins and ends and begins and ends. His eyes listen.

Hey you, watch that fender, careful, don't back the car into the wall; give the paint job some care.

He is rich. He owns a security company in Springs.

You take advantage of whatever comes your way, that's the way of the immigrant, it isn't his home this new place, and so you need to just watch out for whatever opportunity presents itself. I am not an immigrant anymore but my father was, he came from Portugal, and my mother, they came to this country together. But I don't think that you can take the immigrant out of me, it's in my blood, I grew up with it. Hey, people are insecure, people fear that they are, and they will be, preyed upon by those that they do not know, by those that they do not want to know, so they hide behind their walls and their security guards. And I, well I took advantage of this fear. My guards are all trained in the use of hand guns, and some even in the use of the machine gun, this is for mall security, not houses though.

She looks at the security guard that walks up and down outside this building, this secure security building. He supports a gun under an armpit. He is a very big man, he is upright. He whistles to a dog that is chained to a post close to the entrance of the building, an Alsatian, black and brown, a long pointed nose, it is as tall as a child. Alsatian dogs; the dogs trained in the concentration camps, the dogs that ran in the erupting townships.

We have many dogs; they can smell crime, drugs, a lot of them. These dogs they know who the enemy is, they can smell him, they can even smell through the dirt, through deodorant.

I only work for two weeks in a month, the other two weeks I travel. Last week I was in the Maldives, beautiful place. The manager of the place where we, my wife and I, where we stayed, said that last year Kate Moss was there, and that she has great tits, even for her age.

Ja, Springs, it is an interesting community because it has gone through many changes, not a very good change now. I think that the town has changed for the worse. But hey, remember my perspective, I grew up in the apartheid times, the times that many people in Springs, or rather I should say those white people who lived in the town, call the good old days, and so this is what I know. I don't know Congolese and dirt and French and new cheap goods from China sold by Bangladeshis who can't speak English and who have prayer rugs on their shop floors and a sign that points somewhere, where is it, somewhere sacred. I don't know poverty like it is now; it was never in front of me like it is here now, it was always outside, in the townships. My parents, hey, they were poor, that's why they came to this country, the government here was giving all European immigrants a new break, a new start, but I didn't really know poverty, my poor was a different kind. Now it seems to me as if it is a dirty poverty, people don't care, they live behind their shops with only one toilet.

Springs, it is an immigrant town, ja, always has been. Now there are just new immigrants. I don't like them.

The Springs buildings, beautiful hey! Most of them were built in the 40's, at that time it was easy to build these buildings and not expensive, lots of them were built by the Jews. Often they built their shops and then on top was the place that they lived in, that is why if you look at the buildings most of them have shops beneath the apartments. Of course now it is a different kind of shop, no longer the bakery and the haberdashery, now it is fast food and clothes and those general stores that sell everything from gas stoves to TV's. Now the buildings have been taken over by illegal immigrants, lots of them live here, the Jews and all the whites, they left in about 1992, when more blacks started moving in and when the mines started to close down. They, the blacks, don't maintain the buildings. Some of them are even hijacked.

It is a shame.

I think that this place should become something different, it should become a tourist hub, people can leave the airport, which is not far away, and come and look at the buildings. The council should have a vision, they don't, they just let the town go to ruin, but there are more beautiful buildings here than in Miami. I want to start something like this, get a big

company to buy the buildings, fix them up, kick out the people that live there, renovate, make them something that the tourist wants to visit, like Miami, that's what they did there, it used to be a dump, drugs, transvestites, Cubans. They fixed the buildings and now people take tours to look at them, Barbara someone, can't remember her name, persuaded the city of Miami, maybe Dade County, I don't know, but they fixed them up and now look.

You see, listen to me talking, there is still the old immigrant left in me, that old entrepreneurial spirit, that is why I don't go. I might not live here anymore, I live in Benoni, it's better there, cleaner, safer, and it's not that I don't have a choice, like my father, but I stay as I can still make a lot of money.

OK I'll show you around.

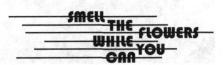

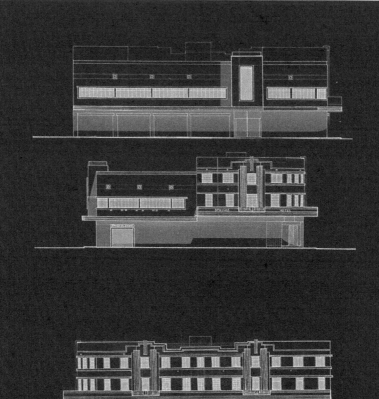

[raffle leaf – a scrolling serrated leaf-like ornament found in
art deco and rococo decorations]

[octastyle – the spiralled columned front of a temple, used often
in art deco, most often it is decorative, but also necessary to
hold up parapets and balconies]

The world is a beautiful place
to be born into
if you don't mind happiness
not always being
so very much fun
if you don't mind a touch of hell
now and then
just when everything is fine
because even in heaven
now and then
they don't sing
all the time
The world is a beautiful place
to be born into
if you don't mind some people dying
all the time
or maybe only starving
some of the time
which isn't half bad
if it isn't you

To: B
From: A
Re: Springs

Did you read of the Warhol-esque ballet performance that was put on at Renesta House? This is that green building on 3rd street, the one which has the four shops beneath it. It is the well-kept building where, when you look at it, the eye is drawn to the orthogonal frames of the windows. The name of the building is written in bold decorative lettering just above the entrance. Apparently a similar performance was put on at the Ocean Drive Carlyle Hotel in Miami? Did you know that Springs has the most Art Deco buildings in it after Miami? The performance was magnificent. The performer of the allegro, this is that brisk, buoyant movement, the performer leaps into the air and stretches his legs while airborne, was dressed as a bird, his wings were made of the art works, copies I suppose, what isn't a copy of a copy of a copy, of Jean Michel Basquiat, he was the artist, Andy Warhol's young and beautiful black project, he died of a heroin overdose at twenty, or was it twenty four? The performer had a scar running down the centre of his face so that, his face that is, was divided in two and only then was one aware that a face is not symmetrical, but anyway after the performance, he sat down on the edge of one of the balconies, the curved one on the third floor of Renestra House and cried. Did you know that allegro means happy? And do you know why he cried? I heard this, or maybe I read it in the brochure that was given out before the performance, apparently because Jean Michel Basquiat is dead and that Springs is not Miami, and that Miami and Springs are both dying, for different reasons. Then he, or maybe it was a she, there was no gender to be discerned, went inside, her face was happy, and she leapt down the stairs stopping at the different stained glass windows, they're green and yellow and red and have a Picasso-esque, design, and mouthing the words 'I am a photograph'. The stained glass windows magnified him and made him different colours depending upon where he was standing. She really was a photograph.

Springs, the space, moves
and jumps, in a brisk and
lively way; its movements are
as quick as it changes; some
say it is disintegrating, others
say magnifying.

This place, it is a picture of a town, what was small and
parochial, never a rainbow or a pot of gold, a brisk and
lively place, an electric storm, it jumps from moment to
moment, from era to era from person to person, from
culture to culture.

It is as black as a storm
cloud, and black is, after all,
all the colours
in a rainbow.

In Springs I am never sure where I am going to or where
I am coming from; all I do is move from image to image,
building to building.

I can hear a scream, listen,
the scream reaches from
inside to outside.

It is the people in Springs that scream for they
have a nostalgia for a dream that never was.

Sometime in the
nineteenth century, a long
time ago, pale and white
not all the colours of the
rainbow, long ago all
movement was in
one direction.
Which direction, what direction?
Upwards.
Downwards.
Homewards.
Nowhere.

A long time ago white male farmers

moved into Ekurhuleni.

The space had no name.

This land is my land/As I went walking on that ribbon of highway/And saw above me that endless skyway/I said/God blessed America (South Africa) for me/This land was made for you and me/This land was made for you and me

The farms were large, very large, and their borders were inaccurately drawn, there was no need for a border, a border is, after all, merely an ersatz line drawn in the sand to keep someone, or something, out, and there was no-one, or nothing, that needed to be kept out of this brotherhood of pilgrims. But sometime, sometime that was far away, when private property was sanctified, and this space was owned ...

Was a high wall there that tried to stop me/A sign was painted said: Private Property/But on the back (black) side it didn't say nothing/God blessed South Africa (America) for me/This land was made for you and me

And so then men drew up the borders. What do you own, my land (and my women)? And the men made accurate borders, correct borders, three government owned farms. Geduld = Patience; Paul Kruger bought this farm, there is no record of what he paid for it, but it was valued by the Landdrost of Heidelberg at one hundred pounds, De Rietfontein = Reed Fountain and Brakpan = a small, brackish lake. And then there was extra land, un-owned land, the land was not belonging/did not belong. And so this extra land was owned by the men.

One bright sunny morning in the shadow of the church/I saw my people/As they stood hungry, I stood there wondering if/God blessed America (or South Africa) for me/This land was made for you and me

And so there was a very odd piece of extra land, there between the three named farms.

The land surveyor who surveyed the farms was named Richard Brookes, Brookes in English is a stream or a spring, and *broeks* in Afrikaans means underwear, but Richard Brookes wanted to be a memory, so he called this place The Springs.

Rupert Brookes was immortalised by a compromise, not by his underwear.

Then coal was discovered in The Springs, and so the space changed.

There grew:

Hotels and general dealers and bars and pimps and prostitutes and gunslingers and apartment blocks and a fire station, and families with children and servants and all those things that a small town needs.

And then gold was discovered in The Springs (on the farm Geduld - be Patient and you will find gold), and more gold and more and then there were:

More hotels and more bars and more general dealers and more apartment blocks and some suburbs with families including mother and father and children, and still only one fire station and more pimps and more prostitutes and, of course, more servants.

There was The Springs, and the space moved into a town called Springs.

And then there was a railway line and a railway station.

And now there is no railway and no coal and no gold; but there are

General dealers and hotels and bars and apartments filled with many people and a fire station that is a monument not a fire station, and pimps and prostitutes and many taxis and many beautiful buildings.

And the gold is movement that is dancing golden.

To: B
From: A
Re: Springs

In South Africa we have the weird and never ending belief in the value of property, I say we even though I know that we means me, or others like me. And this is bizarre as of course it was property that caused the 2008 meltdown, well sort of, I suppose it was the manipulation of the idea of the value of property in America and then there was this ripple effect, and as a consequence there was massive movement; prices, people moving from their homes, children thrown into fires or rivers or the ocean. So much for the value of property, it was stamped on and beaten to death. Anyway we still romanticise property and so all the buildings here are owned by a few people, and they rent them out for a lot of money, mostly to immigrants. There are always a lot of people in the flats. It is interesting how I think that this is a sacrilege. How can so many people be stuffed into such a beautiful space? Art Deco, a western ideal, a beautiful decorative architecture, and yet for others it is just a space that they make into a place. Did you know that the word battu means a movement where the feet beat an extra amount; the beating of feet on the tarmac, the beating of feet to beat someone down, downstairs? And because there are so many people in this building, in the street in front of it there is a lot of battu, many feet are beating. Did you know that to dance once was thought of as to dance off earthly property and into heavenly heaven? Not dance off and die, but dance off and fly. I think that the underlying organising principle of the modern world is to crash, a plane crash, and I am glad that you have not crashed, metaphorically that is, and that you want to beat your feet many times over. The last time, the last long ago time I mean, you said that you were writing. Are you still doing this? If you have some money the Parks Hotel, an Art Deco building that is owned by a Tunisian, is for sale, only two million rand, some would say for nothing? Buy it, what a great place to write in, a writing retreat with all the noise of an African city outside, it will sound like Havana.

I think that the Art Deco buildings
of Springs tell a story?

Bricks
Loops

Circles
Parapets

Does your story have a morality?
Does it need to?

Yes.
Then the buildings have no story
for Art Deco is almost entirely devoid of a social
or moral agenda; it is only style, it embraces the
eclectic and the ornamental, there are colours,
different materials and lustrous surfaces. Art Deco is
consumerism, luxury, excitement and glamour.

Art Deco is the architecture of the future;
the Futurists, Marinetti, the worship of the
machine. Buildings are machines - flying
machines, ships, motor cars.
Buildings tell the story of the machine, but do
machines have stories?

We are against sadness, moonlight
and marriage.
And we hate sentiment, it is real.

We are against the colonial past, this
infatuation with the presence of the past.
We are against tradition, the tradition of culture.

We are against tribalism, symbolism,
moralism, parliamentarianism,
individualism, archaism, egoism, and
pessimism and every kind of materialistic
self-serving cowardice.
We are against the great and famous colonists of the
past, great white men are a very trivial thing.

We will write sounds, noises and smells.
We will free ourselves from the stink of the
professors, archaeologists, tour guides and
historians.

We believe in the movement of ideas.
We want to sing about the love of danger, about the
use of energy and recklessness as a daily practice.

Courage, boldness, and rebellion will
be our poetry.
We will glorify aggressive action,
a restive wakefulness, life at the double,
the slap and the punching fist.

We believe that this wonderful world is
enriched by the beauty of speed; a racing
car, its bonnet decked with exhaust pipes
like serpents with galvanic breath, a roaring
motor car, which seems to race on like
machine-gun fire.
We wish to glorify war,
it is the sole cleanser of the world.

I think that Art Deco is the
architecture of the poet.

Listen: they are a vibrant fervour of spaces that are ablaze with violent
electricity; a fire station that devours smoke-plumed dragons, a hotel
that hangs on clouds by the crooked lines of its balconies, apartments
that stride the streets as giant gymnasts that flash in the sun, the
glitter of threatening knives. It is adventurous players that sniff the
horizon, built like the streets where the motor vehicles' wheels paw
the tar like the hooves of enormous steel horses. It is a sleek flight
of aeroplanes whose propellers chatter in the wind like banners and
cheer like an enthusiastic crowd for the street is made of countless
voices that blend into one high but resonant sound which vibrates on
the ear as if it were trying to penetrate beyond hearing. It will make
the universe crackle and angels dance in the static on designs of
mysterious and romantic animals, the fiery sun and fountains of steel.
It is the wings of aircraft, the portholes of ships and the wheel
of the fast cars.

And the Art Deco buildings
are the stories of people,
it is their poetry; words
of luxury and desire and
prosthetic limbs that
run and dance; tales of
ballerina buildings that
do not teach of morality
but celebrate and make
legends of the children
who live inside them.

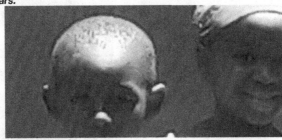

The architecture of a story?

The exquisite, historical, Art Deco apartment buildings are crying out for a canny investor to snap up a few and restore them. It could mean an inner city revival akin to that happening in Joburg.

What an idea, an Art Deco theme park that can provide millions of guests an opportunity to escape from the everydayness of their boring lives. They can enter a world that's better than their own, even if they do live in America and know Miami, this is Miami, without the ocean, in Africa.

Mmmm, yes, we all want to live in an era that is not our own.
And a place that is not our own.

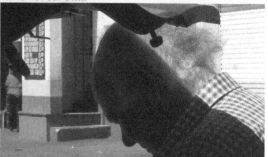

And this town is completely real, because it was real in the 40's and 50's, and now it can be the completely real fake in the 2000's.

The pleasure of imitation, we can imitate the gods, is one of the most innate pleasures of the human spirit; but here, we will enjoy a perfect human imitation, after all where can we go now?

Afterwards reality will always be inferior to this simulation.

Don't get so intellectual; just imagine a busload of foreign visitors traipsing down the street, peering into the buildings, taking a selfie in front of the magnificent entrances? The people that live here are wild, man, think of them like animals in a zoo; the tourist can stare from the outside but, hey, don't dare get too close, can't go inside.

Mmmm, yes, and the visitors won't need to interact, they don't want to; they don't want to be contaminated by the poor, too dirty, they just want their photo op, so contact with locals will be minimal, the nice ones can wave to them.

And the money, will it trickle down to the locals?

Hell no, the operators, that's us, will fill our pockets, tourism profits from poverty. But there will be tourists and that's good isn't it, the economy will profit?

It sounds great, but do you think that people might feel degraded by being stared at while they do mundane things - washing, cleaning up, preparing food, private things? How would you feel?

These tours will make poverty exotic, otherworldly, glamorous, why should what is to an inhabitant not be utilised for profit, my profit and theirs? Do I care that the reality will remain once the tourists are gone? And anyway some money does enter the community, whether through meals in the local eateries, like that guys over there, or the purchase of art or souvenirs, like all this ethnic material, this trickle-down economy is bound to be better for the locals, better than picking trash from a stinking garbage heap, or doing nothing.

Let's do it man.
Yes, let's go for it. I need the money.

The young man wears a light green T-shirt

on which is a picture of Bob Marley; the words underneath this Reggae star are 'No Woman No Cry.' The T-shirt was once a dark olive green, now it is faded to light. Bob Marley is a light brown; his Jamaican darkness is washed out. The young man has a gold tooth, the front right tooth, and dreadlocks that hang onto his shoulders; they are cleanly soiled, he has spent time creating this look. He does not smile, he may not have a woman, no wife or mother, no girlfriend or sister, but just once he did smile, when he heard the red winged starling that sat on the light pole that is on the pavement corner and that had no bulb in it, sing; it whistled, the sound is long and drawn out, spreeeooo, and his tooth flashed for he stands in the sunlight. He points towards the street. He says 'Wait here I will telephone Dennis for you.'

Three men stand at the entrance of a general store, two of them chew, four jaws move up and then they move down, and the third man has a round wad, a ball of something, that seems to be caught in the side of his mouth, he might have tooth ache, or he is eating something that he has not swallowed. In the store on the shelves are chocolates and biscuits and a few potatoes. They all are covered lightly with dust. At the back of the shop four yellow plastic chairs are set around a low metal table, and on the table is a pair of dice, several packets of small green leaves and an empty espresso coffee cup. Above the table a flag hangs from a wooden beam that has been hammered into the dry walled ceiling, it is light blue, the blue of the Indian Ocean and in the centre is a single five point white star, the star of unity, this is the Somali flag. All the men are young; they have light brown skin, dark eyes with small pin prick black pupils, their noses are curved. One of the men, the one who is not chewing, says 'stand at the corner, there, that corner, I will phone Dennis and he will meet you here.'

The inside of the room is cool; there are two fans in it, air blows softly from the left and from the right; the breeze makes the sign of a cross. At the back of the room a cross hangs on the wall, Jesus stares down from it as if at an intruder, his wounds bleed and gasp. On the left an older man in a black suit stands in front of a picture, it is a picture of him, he has greying hair and a small greying beard, in this

picture he looks majestic, God like, better than he does as he stands in this cool room for now he has the smell of old brandy mixed with sheep fat and his eyes are rimmed in red. On the picture are letters, red letters, red capital letters, TCI MINISTRIES, underneath this are words in black, Take Courage Ministries, and below this it says 'Welcome to the House of your Father'. A red winged starling flies across the room, the pink red under its wings flash, and then it flies out again, bird sounds come from a hole in the top right hand wall. The man says 'Welcome, come inside, this is a Christian place, welcome to the house of our Father, it is not safe outside, you can stand here, I will phone Dennis and he will come. He is the only one who can say whether you can go inside the building or not.'

A man walks out of the general dealer shop where the three men who look as if they are Somali are, he walks across the street. He wears a red T-shirt and blue jeans, his Nike boots are scratched and dusty. In an accent that seems French he says 'follow me, those guys over there they will phone Dennis, I have lost my phone and so I don't have his number. But I know those guys, they will phone him.'

Outside the bar, on the wall, is a painted picture of a green and white beer bottle, the words on it are Castle Lite, and above the bottle on a red background in blue capital letters are the words TOP CLUB. Inside the bar there is a snooker table, the green baize is worn in one of the corners, the wood of the table is brown and stained, on the corners many glasses of red wine have been spilled and the netting of two of the pockets is faded and enflamed, crimson and bloodshot. Two balls, a red ball and a blue ball, lie on a nearby table; they have fallen from the broken pocket and been placed there so that they will not get damaged. A black and white dog of no particular breed runs beneath the table, as it does so it kicks at an empty green beer tin which slowly rolls towards the outside door and on towards the pavement, then it rolls into the open drain and disappears. The dog lies down close to the feet of a man; it picks up in its mouth what is left of a chicken bone, then it snaps the bone in two and swallows it, it is gone, it then licks the remains of the gravy and peas that are left in a Styrofoam container. Four men

stand around the snooker table, three of them hold snooker cues, one leans down over the table and holds the blue white tip of the cue to a white ball, another holds a cigarette to his mouth and then, slowly, laconically, blows four smoke rings into the air, the third drinks from a beer bottle, seven gulps, and the fourth speaks into a mobile phone. The man with the phone stops speaking into it, he turns around and says 'Dennis, he will meet you there, down there at the corner.'

The building is Doreen Court, it is painted brown, next door to it is another building; it is made from face brick. The curved balconies of Doreen Court do not stand out, they are not painted another different colour, they fade into the building itself, it is only on a closer look that they are noticeably curved, and, on another closer look, that once they may have been painted an uncommon much lighter colour, food trays emerging from a brick wall. The balconies are now functional rather than decorative, once they were pink and turquoise, now they are brown set against brown, the garbage that piles up on them is rotting. The two front wooden doors to the building are closed; in front of them are locked iron gates, padlocked, the bars are shaped like mermaids, they cannot speak and say what they hold inside them. In the shop on the left hand side of the doors is a sign, it says Christ Kingdom Ministries, but it seems, although the doors are open, that there is no-one there. The shop to the right is closed; the iron gates are also padlocked and evenly browned with dust, the doors have not been opened in a long while. Now there is movement behind the metal gates of the front door, and movement on a balcony, a rat has made its home here, a cat, or is it a person, hidden behind the façade of decoration that is no longer decoration? People shapes pass by the closed and broken panes of glass, a wisp of smoke emerges from an open window, there are cooking smells, meat, and then, quickly, a young girl dressed in sheer stockings and a red and black brassiere, steps out and watches the street from one of the balconies, she waves. A red winged starling, the aging grey of the feathers on its head, sits on the plaster of the balustrade and whistles, it sings to the unclouded sky.

No you cannot go inside the building, no, why, because I say that you cannot, there is a problem with the owner, he does not like it that strangers go inside and I am the caretaker, and I say you cannot go. No, you cannot go inside, I have said this. There is a dispute of ownership with this building so maybe if you come back next time, yes I recognise

you from when you were here before, you were walking down this street, and 3rd street, maybe in three months then the dispute will be finished, the owner will then have no problem with you coming inside, but now no, not now, not today.

Dennis is very dark. He wears a T-shirt that has had the sleeves cut off; it is very white against his very black skin. His biceps have a life of their own when he lifts his arms and reaches upwards to something, what, and then he walks down the pavement. He stops to ask something of someone, a cigarette, then he lights the cigarette that he is given with a golden lighter, a silver platinum bracelet reflects the shadowy word Cartier that is written on the base of the lighter, the flame hisses as he flicks it open, then it is gone, he walks forward, one foot before the other. His shoes are made of brown patent leather, newly polished, burnished, and yet the street is dusty and blackened pieces of paper scud across it in the wind. Dennis is tall, very tall; he is at least six feet tall, and because he stands so upright he appears taller. His head is shaven, there is no stubble on it, and his face is bearded, it is thick, lush, his full red lips smile, a threat, laughter, threatening laughter. He looks down, at everyone, everyone who walks, or stands, for Dennis is very tall.

What does it mean that there is a dispute of ownership?

Ha, do you want to know this, really? I am telling you that there is a dispute and that I am now the owner of the building, there is a problem with the last owner. Look at it, this building, it is dark, dark inside too, and it is falling down, water is running down the walls and there are children inside, they need to have light. Maybe six months ago the city council cut off all the power and the water, there were a lot of people living here and the man, the owner did not care, he just took their money and did not pay for the electricity or water, so it was cut, then they had nothing, it smelled for there are many people here. You can imagine the smell no, and there were rats running about, someone said that a rat nearly killed a baby that was lying on a bed, ate it for the rat was big and the baby was small. Someone told me, I live not far from here, in that other building, yes you have come from there, Coalition House, it is better, the man that owns it cares about the tenants, like me, and the water has not been cut.

Many families live there, no not mine, I have no family and my mother, she is dead, she died before I came here, she was killed by a car. As she was walking down the street a car came driving very fast, she

was trying to cross the street and the car did not slow down, it knocked her and she died, not then, she died later when they were taking her to the hospital but they could not help her because the ambulance was slow, too slow, there are many cars, more than in Johannesburg, often it is better to walk, you get to places much quicker, much quicker than if you drive. But that is my mother, and anyway I came here because here I can make money, a lot of it, and I do make money.

Look at my shoes, Gucci from France, they are new, imported, I buy my clothes from that shop there, there on the corner of Plantation road and 3rd Ave, it does not look as if it has good clothes and shoes but it does, the owner likes to have clients like me, he knows me, that I will always pay, I am one of his good clients, he makes a lot of money from me, and sometimes for me because we do good business, sometimes I have goods that he wants and so we trade. Anyway what is it, yes, I live there, in Coalition House.

I lived for a short time in Johannesburg, in Hillbrow and got a job as a body guard for this guy who worked there also with buildings, he was also a kind of land lord, like I am, he taught me a lot about this business, never let the tenants get away with not paying, with nothing, if they do they think that they can take advantage of you, once they do it one time, not paying, then you must evict them, let them go, you can't take shit from no tenants. Anyway I also worked in a club in Hillbrow, actually it was closer to Berea, it used to be a hotel and then they turned it into a night club, the whole place, even the rooms could be used by some of the people that came to the club. I was hired by the guy who was the landlord to be the bouncer and the body guard there, that is where I learnt to dress well, a bouncer must always must dress well because to be well dressed scares people, and you want to make them scared so that they will not cause trouble. Then I came here, I got into a fight with the guy that I worked for there, he said that I had taken away some of his clients, but I don't know this, how could I have done this? What clients did he have? And how could I have taken them? What did he sell, what did I sell? We did not sell the same stuff.

Where do you work? Why do you want me to tell you this stuff? No you can't go into the building until the dispute is resolved, until I fix it with the owner. Anyway the owner he did nothing and so I said to many people that I know, why don't you all come to Doreen Court and move in. I can get the water fixed up and the electricity, there is no problem to connect it up again. And so some, not all of them, they moved in, and they pay the rent and so there is water now and electricity. No I just need to clean it, then it will be good, a good building to live in.

It is better here in Springs, there are not so many people like Hillbrow and here people they all know me, and they all respect me. I can get them things, things that they need, I know where to buy the khat, the leaves that the Somali and Ethiopian people chew, I know where to find it, I get it from the Somalian people in Johannesburg, but many are moving here now, many of them are here, and I get other stuff, it is a good business.

And yes, yes, the dispute will soon be over, I know what I have to do, then everything will be fine here in Doreen Court and you can go inside. Just come back in three month maybe.

The young man in the Rastafarian T-shirt winks and says 'Dennis says you cannot go inside. You must not go inside.'

The Somalian man who chews khat says 'Dennis says you cannot go inside. You must not go inside.'

The snooker player in the Top Club winks and says 'Dennis says you cannot go inside. You must not go inside.'

The man of Christ in the TCI Ministries says 'Dennis says you cannot go inside. You must not go inside. Jesus will look after Dennis, he is a good man.'

As Dennis walks away a red winged starling flies low above his head, under its wings the feathers are red, obsidian, a shadow falls across his forehead, bisects it, a wound.

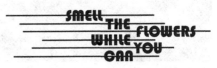

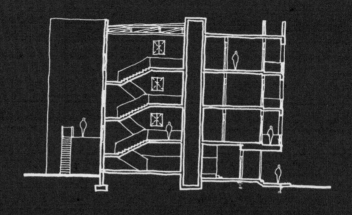

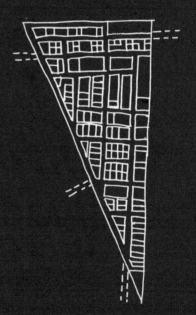

[mullion – a vertical bar that divides an aperture; in art deco it is
sometimes for aesthetic reasons, other times because
the structure requires the cross beams to be held upright]

Among twenty golden minedumps.
The only moving thing
Was the eye of the blackbird.
And on the road we met a blackman.
But no one else.
From the brown paper bags on the pavement
A blackman fills the vacancies of morning
With orange speculations.
Always I hope to find
The blackman I know.
Or one who knows him.
I was of three minds,
Like a tree
In which there are three blackbirds.
The blackbird whirled in the autumn winds.
It was a small part of the pantomime.
The fingerprints of a blackman
Were on her pillow. Or was it
Her luminous tears? An absence, or a presence?
Only when it was darker
Would she know.
I do not know which to prefer.
The beauty of inflections
Or the beauty of innuendoes.
The blackbird whistling
Or just after
The blackman sipped water
From an iron tap.

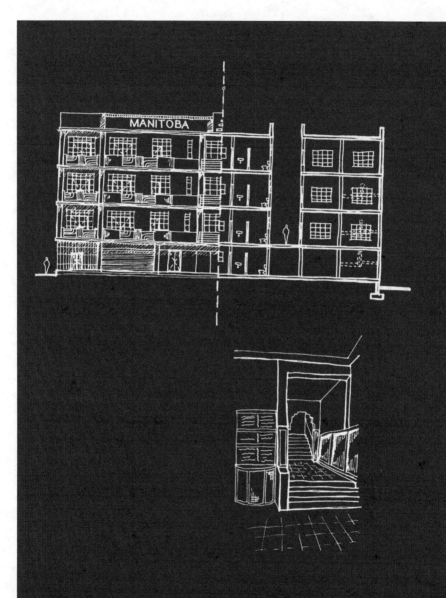

[rectilinear – the composition of the vertical and the horizontal
elements of a building, most often used in the art deco style]

[quoins – the cornerstones of an art deco building,
composed of a different material
from that of the building itself]

And when the tap stopped flowing.
He dipped his hand into the cool blackness
of the bowel.
We are told that the seeds
Of rainbows are not unlike
A blackman's tears.
There is the sorrow of blackmen
Lost in cities. But who can conceive
Of cities lost in a blackman?
The stream is moving
The blackbird must be flying
By moonlight
We tossed our small stones into the slime dam
And marvelled
At the beauty of concentric sorrows.
You thought it was like the troubled heart
Of a blackman.
Because of the dancing light.
As I remember it.
The only unicorn in the park
Belonged to a blackman
Who went about collecting bits
And torn scraps of afternoons.

What does it mean that there is a dispute of ownership, I mean who would want to own such a building, let alone get into a dispute about it?

Don't you know what he was saying?

No, I don't know what he was saying?

He is saying that he hijacked the building?

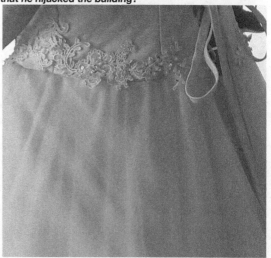

44

So then the
resolution of the
dispute, what does
he then mean?

He means that the owner will be killed, get a bullet in his head unless he leaves town. I think that he was laughing at you. But he likes to be able to tell a story, to craft the way you think of him, create the image that he wants you to think, a romantic Nigerian Robin Hood.

Everything is
disguised as
something else.

Radios are bookcases, a bed is a cocktail cabinet, a story is a tape recording of your voice, a bronze woman who is naked lights a cigarette lighter.

Three people, a white woman with silver hair,

a black woman whose head is shaven and an Asian man who wears large black rimmed glasses, he may be Chinese, or Taiwanese or Vietnamese, sit on a wooden bench outside the Burger Deluxe in Springs; or it is the Casbah in Brakpan?

It is 2019, but it could be 1963, or 1953, only the colours in the spaces have changed.

This is a place from a long time ago.

On the wall of the road house is a name, Casbah, but this is only readable if you walk in front of it and carefully look up, it is made up of faded orange letters that are set in relief on a faded grey wall, diamond shaped designs surround the letters, sculptures in different shades of grey, some dark and some light, but all are grey. The Burger De Luxe, the name is set into bright bright neon lights, they are not lit up now for it is midday and the sun is bright; brighter than neon, and the lead fluorescent light strips are damaged, shattered.

Where are they now?

All three of them look, they look up, look around, look at whom and what is there for it is foreign to them, not something that they know, or are used to; it is another place in another time.

The young Asian man holds up a mobile phone, must have a selfie here.

It is too hot to sit in the car, as you should at a road house; sit in the car and flash the car lights for attention, then have a tray hooked to the open window by a man in a white peaked hat and a red apron. But it is too hot, and the men that serve the road house clients are not dressed in red and white, they wear jeans and T-shirts.

How about lunch?

What do you think they have here, doesn't look all that salubrious?

Well we can always have the good old-fashioned cheese and tomato toasted sandwich on white bread, which is really cheese spread with a few thickly sliced tomatoes, and of course the ubiquitous coke? Even if we don't sit in the car we must have a coke. Let's get the performance right.

Probably have gherkins mixed in with the tomato.

Get the arteries clogged up, ugh!

The white woman laughs, more of a giggle really, behind her sunglasses she stares at this strange place, then the black woman also laughs, and the Asian man takes

a photograph of himself, then, surreptitiously, by holding the phone facing himself and at arm's length as if he is taking another of himself, or the two women who are with him, takes another photograph; a photograph of an old woman and an old man, old in years and old in clothing, both the style, a tent dress and grey wide trousers, and the thin-ness of the material, it is fraying in places, a hole in an elbow or a knee and the socks that are on feet in sandals have holes in them.

Ja, no, we have just come to town today to visit the doctor, Doctor Olivier. We went to the doctor this morning, he used to be in Springs, down here in 3rd street, but he has moved, too many people in Springs now, too many black people. No, he does see blacks, if they have money, they must pay cash, the full price, but he wants to be in a white place for his offices, he thinks that it is better, and more safe, and his patients like it too, they like it that he has moved out of town, it's not safe to drive there in Springs anymore.

We came from Standerton. Ja it's far away. We live there now. We used to be in Springs, down Plantation street in a house, it was good then when we lived there, not so many people, and not so dirty. The schools were just for whites so the children had good education. That's where the children grew up, where we made the family. We were married young, I was mos only seventeen, and Jacob, he was nineteen. Ja, two sons and one daughter. My sons, the one lives in Edenvale in Johannesburg, and the other went with his company to Australia, sometimes he phones, he says it is a good place Australia, he lives in Perth, they even speak Afrikaans there and have biltong. Both of my sons, yes they are both married, no, the one is divorced, the one in Australia, but then he married another woman, an Australian. My daughter, Dulcie, she lives in Standerton now, with her husband and her children. Her husband works there in a place that fixes cars, like a scrap place, and my daughter, she stays at home. No she doesn't work, no work for white people anymore, and anyway she stayed at home and looked after the children, she didn't want a girl there looking after the children. No, they steal and it's too dangerous, you never know they might send their friends in and murder everybody if they know where you live, you know how it is with them. And then she got

old and so couldn't get a job, ja she tried but she couldn't find one, she wanted to work at the Municipality but they only employ blacks now.

We can't live here now, too expensive, and we don't have any money. My husband, ja him, he worked on the mines out there near Springs, here this was his mine worker ticket, look, I have kept it for history, look, it was there, the East Rand Proprietary Mines, they called it by the initials, ERPM, it was the deepest mine in the world they told us, and the gold was good, very good, pure, the best in the mines, good quality, so Jacob was lucky to work there. Now it is closed, it closed in 2008, things were tough then, but Jacob, he had already been retired. You must look at the mine dump, it's next to the highway, it's called Carson or something, I can show you where it is, it is also the highest in the world, but now it is not so high because they are fixing it to make it go away. People still try to get gold from it but there are electric fences around it, and dogs, security men with dogs. Ja, Jacob, he never says anything because he got deaf because of all the blasting in the mine. He is not so old, seventy five, I'm seventy four, but they put him off long ago, when he was fifty, because he could not hear well and he coughs a lot, but also he smokes. They said it was too much pressure in his ears; and the lungs, the blasting caused these problems in his ears and lungs, but he never stopped smoking, still he smokes and coughs, spits too, a lot. You can't tell that he was made deaf in the mine, or that from the blasting he gets a lot of headaches and dizziness, but he was too when they put him off. They were very good to us; they said that even if they could not notice, or the doctors couldn't tell that Jacob was deaf from the blasting they would give him a pension. And Jacob, he was not greedy, not like they are now, they all want to get money from the mines, for TB and stuff, but not Jacob, he was grateful that they were good to him when he worked there, and with the pension. But the pension, it did not last for a long time, so now it's gone. When it was finished I had to get a job, I worked in the OK Bazaars down here in 3rd Street, it was a big shop, worked at the tills, now the shop isn't there anymore, but anyway its only black girls that work on the tills now. We have to get the government pension; it's nothing, not enough, so we have to live with the daughter.

Ja, we live out there on a small plot, just outside the dorp, and my daughter she is there on her own all the time. She watches television, but these days there is not a lot of it for her you know, not a lot, but she does like

Sewende Laan, TV 1, ja that one she likes. I like it too. It's like when I was young but there are more blacks in the films.

Ja, look here look at this picture. Remember Jacob, ag he can't hear me, remember this building, it's where the bioscope is, sometimes also they had plays there, people from the town you know wanted to act. It is a car parts place now? I didn't know, what it is called, CNN motor spares, it's like the place where my son-in-law, Dan, works, but it looks better, his is all scrap metal and broken cars, this looks like a shop. It looks clean too, not like his scrap yard, dirty, all those old pieces of cars, and he never cleans it, and there is a lot of grease everywhere, old oil from the engines. You say Indians own it, well you know Indians are clean people, they are always washing, it's good, not like the blacks. The building, ja I think it was the old bioscope you know, we used to go to the films there, some dirty films, not Afrikaans, American.

Marlene, you can nie nee se, you can't say no, this is the first time that we can go out alone. Pa, he says I can take you out, and your ma, she says the same, so let's go to the bioscope. And you can trust me. Both your ma and pa know this, they know that I don't drink a lot. What is the film at the bioscope?

Why you want to go there? I don't like the films that they show there, not always, well maybe just sometimes.

I like to go, it's dark inside anyway.

Ja, my pa says that it's OK, but that I must be home before 10 o'clock. He won't know if I am late, but he says 10, he will be drunk by then, but still it's 10 o'clock, and ma will be waiting for me, she always waits up for me, I know.

We can go to the road house, and then to the bioscope. The film starts at past seven, and we can go to the road house before for a lekker hamburger. I can take a beer from pa, he won't know. And my boet says that I can take the car even though I don't have a licence proper, can only get it next year but I can drive, and it's not far anyway.

Don't tell my Pa that you don't have a licence; he won't let me go with you then. Just don't say anything, and if he asks, say your brother is driving. Also don't tell him about the beer.

What's the film?

Some Like it Hot, I think that is what it is called. Theunis, the moffie manager at where I work says that it is a good film. He says that it is very popular in Joburg; it's about a lady and two men who dress up as ladies. I don't know, I am not sure that I want to go to a film about men that dress as ladies; it is

like not right, God never said that men can be women. But Theunis, you know him, the one who always wears those grey shoes, and the shirt with the flowers on it, the moffie man, you know him, the one that shouts a lot and speaks strange, he said that it was funny, so maybe it will be nice. And anyway there isn't anything else to do.

Ja, and when the lights are off. Remember the other day when we were at your house and your pa and ma had gone to bed?

I remember and it's not going to happen, I don't like it, and God doesn't like it also. We can't do it, Jacob, not now, not until maybe we get married.

So what did he say about it, Theunis, about the film?

It's got that American lady in it, Marilyn Monroe; she has white hair and is very pretty. And it's about robbers, the men have to dress up as ladies because otherwise they could be caught, there are some bad guys after them, they want to murder them, I think that is what it is about. And the lady, Marilyn Monroe, she falls in love with one of them, I think, but she can't, she can't fall in love with a lady, don't know, but anyway Theunis says that it is funny. But then he likes to wear the shirts that could be a dress so I don't know.

Ja I have heard of her. All the ou's have the hots for her. There is that picture when she is standing above a drain and her skirt is blowing up, the poster outside the bioscope, the guys put it on the wall at the garage. And she was going with the American President someone told me and the President is married. OK I'll come by your house at 5 and then we go to Burger De Luxe for the hamburger and then we go there.

Ja OK.

Hey, hey!

Yes.

I notice that all of you are walking around and taking pictures of the building. My name is Nevin, my family owns this building, it used to be the old theatre or the movie house, and if you want to I will show you inside.

Yes, we would like that, great. Your mother, I think it was your mother, she said in addition to your shop, there is an upstairs area that is rented to a Nigerian ministry, and that we could go inside if they are there, but they aren't. So thank you.

No it's not their part of the building that I want to show you, it's the back of the shop where we are, behind the shop. I'll show you what is there, we have to walk through our part. There are pictures there that have been painted on the walls and all the old pillars of the theatre are still there. I want to fix it

up some day, make it a place that people can come into. Maybe even show films here again. We can still have the shop, but it will be great if it is fixed. Come in, come. No just follow me; we will go to the back, past all this stuff.

Inside the movie theatre it is dark. As the eye adjusts the dark blue paint on the bottom of the walls becomes visible, sapphire, cerulean, wealth, indulgence and fantasy. Above this the walls are carved and patterned, an almost Grecian design, women and men, tall, God-like, walk upwards and out of the walls, in relief, a church, pagan exoticism.

Nevin stands on a box, a soap box, an old wooden chair, he points upwards and to the side, he gestures and bows, this is his directorial debut.

To the right is another long wall, yellow and white and red boats sail on a sea of blue water. Below the paintings and below the God like reliefs the wooden parquet floors are covered with broken pieces of metal and plaster and bricks, unnerving and creepy. Who lingers in this theatre now, what did they do as they watched a flickering screen, men as women, a blonde goddess, the audience is silent now, just the flicker of a sound in the corner, laughing, holding hands, making out in the dark, the painted boats on blue water, a coke machine whines, a popcorn machine pops; young girls in short socks and flowered dresses, young men in khaki shorts with greased back hair. Ghosts that watch the voyeurs take their photographs, photographs that will remember, a recording of the long dead; now is another time, another audience.

What fears and needs and hopes and dreams hide in the corroding floors?

Ja, we have to go back to Standerton today. My daughter just dropped us here because my husband, hey Jacob, Jacob, he can't hear very well, deaf, it's the old age and the blasting and we don't have money, I said we live on the government pension. It was better then, the blacks weren't the government. We had a better life then. But maybe it was because we were young and now we are old. I don't know if I really had a better life then, if I even had a life. My daughter and her husband they are always complaining, complaining about the dirty towns and all the blacks. I complain too, but I think that I complain because everyone is complaining. I don't have anything else to do.

But I do remember that film place. It was the bioscope that we all went to because it was so dark when they turned the lights off and also because they would also show

these films from America. Sometimes they were dirty, but we still went. It was good those times. I was pretty then.

Hey Jacob, don't sleep man, we have to wait for Dulcie she said that we must wait here, and it's a nice day to be outside. Careful man. Tell these people about Springs when you were younger. No he won't speak to you, he can't talk English so well and anyway I told you he is deaf.

My daughter, no she never went to the bioscope in Springs. Maybe she did, I can't remember how old she was when she got married and moved away, it was before things were getting bad here, so she maybe did go to the bioscope, I can't remember. Ja I have ten grandchildren and three great grandchildren. Four of my grandchildren live in Australia with my one son, the divorced one, they live there with their mother, well three do, I think they still stay with her, Esme, ja she was nice, a nice girl, my son, he married again and his new wife has also got a child with him. Three of them live in Edenvale with my other son, but they never visit so I don't know them so well. And the ones that live with my daughter, in Standerton with me and Jacob also, they are twenty and twenty one, you know she couldn't have children after that, something went wrong and she had to have an operation, then Dulcie she got very fat, they both stay with all of us, and the boy works with his father in the scrap metal place, the place with all the cars that I told you about. But he doesn't like it, he is lazy and he is a moffie, a poofter you know them, and he hates working there with his father. He says that he wants to have a sex change or something, he says a lot of people are doing this now, they are born into wrong bodies, that's what he says, his name is Charl but he likes to call himself Lily, Lily is like a flower, a pansy. I don't know, I just keep quiet because what can I do, nothing, but to me it's against nature, against God. My granddaughter she wants to be a teacher, she wants to teach small children, so she goes to the Boston College in Klerksdorp. It's a good college; they have them in Johannesburg too. She comes back to Standerton on the weekends. She doesn't have a boyfriend, my daughter says that it is good because she should not get married too young, like me, and like her, she wants her to be a teacher and make money, then she can help us too. But also she knows what it's like to be married, a lot of hard work, and you can't do what you want to do. Jacob, he never hit me, but Dan, sometimes he gives Dulcie a good klap, I don't blame him, she can cause problems, doesn't like to cook

you know, but she says that she doesn't want her daughter to be married like she was, too young you know, like me, too young, and I was pretty then.

A red car, an old 1950's model Chevrolet, an Art Deco piece of motor art, is parked in the shade just beyond the road house. The car is long and sleek, there are wing-shaped prows on the back of it, and headlights stare out between a metal V, round eyes on the red ocean. The car seems as if it was painted yesterday, there are no scratches on it and the red paint gleams. An old man with an open bald patch on top of his head and long white curly hair and who wears a blue and white checked shirt stands next to it. He walks around the car and opens the bonnet, the engine shines and the silver metal work reflects the road house sign, Casbar, a mirror. The man looks inside it for a while, ten minutes go by and he does not raise his head. When he does oil streaks the side of his face and cuts across his thin pale lips, his face is mottled pink from years of sun and alcohol and weariness. He reaches into his pocket and takes out a piece of cloth; then again he leans into the engine and wipes away a black stain, a shell shaped oil stain from the Niger Delta. Then he holds up his left hand to shade his face, or to wipe away the oil; he has two fingers missing from his hand, the thumb and the index finger, on the fourth finger he wears a gold wedding band.

Ja, I have a lot of these old cars, come to my place it is in Plantation Street. I have a big yard with all the cars you can look at them. But you must phone me before you come, I keep dogs, pitbulls and you know those dogs, if they don't know you, they get savage, they once attacked the garden boy because he was wearing something different to what he normally wears, I had to take him to the hospital, and look, look at my hand. They are not fighting dogs, but they are brutal enough. No-one, no-one comes onto the property, the dogs make them afraid. Oh ja, the cars, I only drive them out sometimes not all the time, mostly on the weekend, mostly when I bring my grandchildren here to the road house or we are going somewhere else, it's nice for them to get out, and I like it too because I live alone there, the wife died five years ago, cancer. There they are, the two kids, there with the mother, my daughter in law, my son, he works at the security place there in Springs, the one the Portuguese guy owns, he works mostly in the day but also at night. This car, it's like the cars that used to be in Springs before now. I'll show you some pictures of the place, the main street with all

the old cars in it. The Portuguese guy, he has
a lot of the pictures, I remember he asked me
for some that I had, he wanted to put them
on the computer so I gave them to him. Ja,
I like to look at the pictures, those were the
good days, the days when we could go
walking into town and not be worried, it's
different now, worse. And all the blacks are
in the shops, and the OK has gone, so has the
big chemist that was owned by Basie Smit,
Hoppies. Ja, ja. But I like these old cars, they
take me back when I drive them, like this one,
I used to drive it with my girlfriend, she was
not my wife, no I never married her. She
married another guy, then she had a child,
maybe eight months after they were married,
and they said it was premature, ja it was a
small kid when it was born, never grew very
tall, like a dwarf.

OK come to my house and you can look
at the cars then. The boy is bringing your
food so come sometime, I am always there.

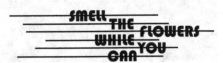

[spolia – the re-use of existing or ruined buildings so as to create new ones, often art deco was the decoration of old buildings]

[sill – the horizontal base of the window, used predominantly in an art deco building]

Chike came from Lagos far away. Hitch-hiked.
(walked, drove a car, caught a train), his way
across the oil fields/war zones/national parks to
come and stay. Plucked his eyebrows on the way,
shaved his legs and then he was a she. She said,
hey babe, take a walk on the wild side, said, hey
honey, take a walk on the wild side.
Jean Claudette came from Kinshasa on the river.
In the backroom she was everybody's darling. But
she never lost her head, even when she was giving
head. She said, hey babe, take a walk on the wild
side. She said, hey babe, take a walk on the wild
side.
And the coloured girls go,
Doo doo doo doo doo doo doo doo doo (x6)
Doo doo doo doo doo doo doo doo doo doo
Little Ahmed never once gave it away. Everybody
here had to pay and pay. A hustle here and a hus-
tle there. Springs is the place where they say hey
babe, take a walk on the wild side. I said hey
Ahmed, take a walk on the wild side.
Sugar, a magic fairy, came and hit Plantation
Street, looking for soul food and a place to eat.
Went to the Springs Hotel, you should have seen
him go: go, go, go. They said, hey Sugar, take a
walk on the wild side. I said, hey babe, take a
walk on the wild side, alright.
Jenny is just speeding away. Thought she was
Denzil Washington for a day. Then I guess she had
to crash, crack would have helped that bash. She
said, hey babe, take a walk on the wild side. I
said, hey honey, take a walk on the wild side.
And the coloured girls say .....

For many years I lived in Lagos.

Banjoko, a slum area, want to know what this word, what Banjoko, means in English, don't ever leave me. Ha don't ever leave me, you lucky if you can ever leave. Slum, what do I say, it is a slum, no it's not something like a shanty town, it's not a shanty town, it's a slum. It is dirty, lots of garbage, white plastic bags that get caught in the fences, they look like small ghosts as they are white and the rest of the place is dark brown, and they always move cause it is windy, many brick houses, falling down, houses made of tin that are on fire as they are so hot. The sun beats on them and then they get hot and then the heat just stays inside. You can roast a chicken without lighting a fire if you leave it inside for an afternoon. We lived, my mother, brother and my two sisters in a brick house, but it is an old one. It was already not in a good condition when we moved in; my mother told me this because I was born in this house. One bedroom, we shared the sitting room to sleep in, we would put the blankets behind the couch in the day time. There is a picture on the wall. I took it from a calendar that I found somewhere, a forest, green tall trees; I think it is in America. Many years I lived there with my mother and brother and two sisters, I told you this didn't I, I repeat myself a lot these days, maybe I just want to remember the words of that place. Anyway my sister, she died when she was fifteen, killed by some gang member, there were gangs that lived in the slum, they didn't want to leave, the name suited them, don't ever leave, they did well with selling drugs and fighting. Ha, I can see your face, all Nigerians sell drugs. Well no, not all, only some do, like everywhere and everyone, and even the drug dealers, they are people too, even sometimes they feel sad and cry. It's boring I know but they do have mothers and fathers and sometimes they love other people, care about them, and they get sick and die just like anyone else. Life is cheap, isn't that what you say, easy to be born easy to die. Once I sat on the beach in Lagos, went there for a day with my friend, Angie, she called herself Angie, it sounded American. We were sitting in the beach bar, oh yes we knew where we could sit and not pay. And then a body got washed up out of the sea; a body. It was lying there on the sand, right next to us. It was big and black, bloated. They came to fetch it later, took it away on a stretcher.

And there were some kids playing next to us. Cheap, life in Lagos is cheap. But what was I telling you? Yes, sometimes people got in the gang crossfire. My sister, she was killed one day when she was just walking across the road to visit her friend, not even for drugs or anything like that. Not sure, maybe it was a mistake, maybe not. She was one of the gang member's wives. I don't mean that they were really married, what we call girlfriends, so maybe someone wanted her dead to punish that guy. I can't even remember his name, her name was Binyelum, can't remember his name, did I even know it, I can't remember. Actually I can't remember what she looked like either.

Life, if you are poor, is cheap. Anywhere. And if you are poor it's easy to die.

My mother always said that there was a world outside Banjoko, somewhere far away. All I had to do was find it. She said I would find it in my dreams. But I didn't want to just dream. So every day I walked down the main road, it is called the Sandayo road, to the railway station to look for this way because I didn't only want to find it in my dreams. It's a long road, Sandayo. It is tar, but with holes in it, and many people and cars. Sometimes I would get work in the small shop that sold cigarettes and videos, Nigerian videos, knock- offs and Nollywood stuff at the station, and other times I would just hang out there and watch the people get on and off the trains. The trains came into the station only two times a day, but every time they came, or every time I watched, some of the people looked so elegant. Not all of them were like this, there were some who just hung on the sides of the train and they were dirty and they made me afraid, even some of the third class ones made me afraid. But the people who got off from the first class, there were a few of those, they were the well-dressed ones, they wore suits even though it was very hot. Mostly it was men, but some women, sometimes. I think the men came for the women, there were a lot of whores in Banjoko, but maybe not; maybe they had family there, a mother or a father, I don't know. I liked to watch the trains, they were old. One day I would get on one, get into first class with a handsome man and go somewhere, somewhere else, go somewhere that was out of Banjoko. One day I wanted to be lifted out of there, lifted out by someone

great, and of course, they must be unknown to the police, so I would be free.

Then a man got off the train. He was very tall and I thought he was very handsome, but maybe this was just because he looked rich. He might be able to get me out of here, I thought. He was pitch black, not like me, I am brown, he was black. He was big, very big. He had a gold tooth in the front of his mouth, I think it was his left front tooth. It's the fashion to have a gold front tooth, expensive too. He came to me and started to talk, we talked for a long time, then he took me to the station café for lunch, just a sandwich, I remember it was a goat's meat sandwich; it had two pieces of tomato in it. He said we should be friends so I went with him to his friend's place that was close by and had sex with him and he gave me some money. From that day I met him often; I think I knew that he would be that great bird that would lift me out of Banjoko. One day he said that if I take a package for him to South Africa I could stay there, he would get me a passport and a visa to go there and then after that what I did I did. He wanted to know nothing more. If I stayed there I stayed there and if I wanted to come home well there was the return air ticket that I could use. And the package, all I had to do was put it at the bottom of my suitcase, near my wash bag and all the soap powder that I needed to wash my clothes for the journey. Then when I got there I would give it to a taxi driver who would come up to me and say something to me in Yoruba, *iranti*. Memory, *iranti* means memory, maybe he thought I would remember him so this is why he chose the word *iranti* as the code word, or maybe he knew that I would never come back so should always remember Banjoko. He said I would be safe as he knew people in South Africa and that because of this they would not take me aside and search my bag.

Maybe he did not really like me, was not my friend, he must have been watching me for a long time because he picked me out, and there were a lot of girls who just hung out at the station. But then maybe he was my friend as I think he noticed that I was hungry, hungry to get out of this slum. I trusted him. He was my big feathered bird.

I never knew his name.

He told me to meet him at the airport in three weeks and he would give me the air ticket and the money and the package.

What did I have to lose, only the daily walk down Sandayo road? I did not want all my journeys to take place on the Sandayo road, I did not want my journeys to be just up and down the Sandayo road because this route never changes.

And so three weeks later I walked down the Sandayo road for the last time, but because I was walking it for the last time it looked different and felt different, and I was going somewhere, not just to the station. And then at the bottom of the road I caught a bus, then another bus and then a taxi to the airport. He, the man, gave me money for the taxi but not for new clothes or anything like that. I met him at the place where he said he would be. Did I say that I did not know his name? He gave me my air ticket and some money, American dollars, I have never had American dollars before, they are green and very valuable, and the package. In the package there were lots of small packages. I opened my own suitcase and carefully packed the small packages that were in the big package into my suitcase, not just in one place, I spread them out, even though the man said it was not a problem as he knew people at the airport in Johannesburg, I think I said that to you too, and they would not talk or call me over, but just to be certain I spread them out. In this way they would be hidden from the X Ray machines, and the dogs, he told me that there are drug-sniffing dogs at the Johannesburg airport.

Of course I knew that I was taking drugs. Of course I know that I am the Nigerian story, the one Nigerian story that you all know, but there is more to me you know, there are more stories that I can tell you. I am not just one story. What do you want to know? I will tell you what you want to know. The Nigerian story, ha, my story, ha.

A bit later I got onto a plane to Johannesburg but as I was early, or at least I had to meet the man with the gold tooth early, I had a lot of time to walk around the airport. It is such a big place and there were so many people in it. They all looked different, different tribes I think, but also different like in clothes and colours, they must have been from all different places in the world, and there were so many shops. I had enough money, I took some from one of my brothers, I don't care that I stole from my brother, he made his money by stealing anyway, so I didn't care and I got some from the man with the gold tooth. I just went into all the shops and looked at the clothes and smelt the perfumes and stole some chocolate. I ate it for lunch. I also bought myself some perfume, no, it's finished now, but it smelt like some sort of flower, sweet like when a piece of sugarcane is cut, but not so sweet that you want to eat it, you just want to lick it. Maybe I bought it as if I put it on someone would want to kiss me on my

skin where I sprayed it. And I had to buy it with one of the dollars, or rather one of the pieces of paper that the man gave me, almost to say to myself this is just paper, and I can swop paper for perfume. Then I had to get on the plane. I was so excited that I did not sleep, I just watched the clouds go by. I have only ever watched clouds from the ground, from the Sanjoko road. From the road they are grey and sad and they hold the heat in. In the sky they are silk, silky against the blue sky, soft.

In Johannesburg airport I joined the queue that said African nationals and just walked through the passport control. It was a long queue. I didn't understand a lot of what people were saying, there were lots of different languages. Then I collected my suitcase and just walked through the customs. No-one stopped me; they did not even look at me. Then I walked into the airport, someone told me that it is named after a hero in the South African fight for freedom. I like that they honour their freedom fighters. And then I met the taxi driver. I remember him calling me, he said *hey girl, eyi ni egbe egan, omokunrin, omokunrin, eye ni egbe egan*, it means hey girl, this is the wild side, hey boy, this is the wild side, in Yoruba. And then he whispered *iranti* I walked together with him outside and to his car. He said that he would take me wherever I wanted to go.

I opened my suitcase and gave him the packages, I kept one for myself and he didn't notice this, and then I said to him I don't know this city. He said, Ok I'll take you to Springs, it is smaller but still close by. And so here I am. I sold the package that I kept to a white guy who came into the hotel where I work. It was enough for the deposit for the room that I have in that building over there, the one with the red paint, Manitoba House. I have a room; it costs only R1400.00 a month. There is a bathroom that is always clean, it's down the passage. There are some good people who live there, they don't hate Nigerians. And the kids there are cute; they like it that I give them popcorn, it's good for you, popcorn, not like chocolate, good for digestion. And I always give them money, Nigerian money, not valuable here, it looks like mystery money.

I love the building, I love how the balcony curves, it like wraps around a body, my body when I sometimes stand outside and look at the street, it is as if it just hugs me close to the brickwork. It is my place, I never bring clients home, they stay there, at the hotel, this is my place, for only me. Sometimes my boyfriend comes round, he is Tunisian, but he does not live here, I don't want him to live here, I

like being alone sometimes. He has shown me pictures of Tutankhamen, the Egyptian pharaoh that died very young and whose tomb was found by some archaeologists. Egypt is close to Tunisia, that's how my boyfriend knows about this. My building reminds me of the pictures of Tutankhamen, his mask in death, it is not gold and blue it is red, but the way the curves look is the same. And look at the way the walls stretch into a point, someone told me that it is built like a pyramid carved out of stone. And look, look at these circles of steel on the railing of the stairs, circles of stainless steel, Tutankhamen's eyes. And look, look there at the side, it flies, that there, that part, is the wings. My boyfriend says that the dead pharaohs flew out of their bodies and into the spirit world. I sometimes do this when I sit on the balcony and look at the sky.

I like it here. It is great. I have never left since the day the taxi driver dropped me here. And every day I make money, some days more and some days less. Every day I walk down Plantation Road from my flat in 3rd Avenue, the time is mostly the same time every day, and every night I walk back home, sometimes late and sometimes early. I earn enough money to have a good time. I like this town. And there are many people here who come from Lagos, only one other from Banjoko though and I never knew her before. And it is safe, people don't really give me trouble, they know me now.

Why do you ask if I miss Banjoko? No, I don't.

Why do you ask if I miss my mother? No, I don't.

I don't miss anything.

Lagos is just another place.

I don't cry for home because this, this is my home. Why would I think of Banjoko as home, it isn't?

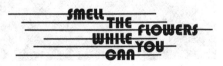

I'm Kamohelo, ha they call me the latchkey kid.

That is what the guy who brought all the white people said I was, he was tall and all the white people were following him and listening to him. I don't know what he was telling them, but they listened and they took photographs. No, they never came inside, not like you; I think that they thought it was too dirty and they would get sick. I was standing outside because it was Sunday and all the people, and my mother, are sleeping so early on a Sunday. It was cold, I remember because the man asked me if I was cold. I'm six. How old are you? You look old. I don't know old people, my mother she's young. She works on a Saturday night at the Kentucky Chicken that place over there and they stay open late because many people buy it on a Saturday, I think because they like to eat and get drunk. She always brings us this chicken, I like it.

Look, look here, it's fake money. Mandela's not on it, it must be fake.

I live here with my mother, only her, no not my father, we don't know where my father is, and my mother, she is at work today, yes at the Kentucky Chicken, that's why I am alone. It's school holidays, that's why I am here, normally when it is not holidays I am at school. Lucky, if I wasn't here then I could not show you where I live. Come, look, it's down here, down this passage. Just hold this the key is here, won't you help me, that's it, yes, no, that's fine I can turn it now.

I go to the school down the road; it's called Selcourt Primary school. I'm in Grade two; the teacher there says that I am smart and cool.

Do you want me to show you where I live? Come. We live in this room, we have a big TV, and the bathroom; it's here, a bit down the passage, we share it with her, that girl there, and her brother, he is my friend; sometimes he is my best friend, Sphesihle. Her name is Londiwe, she is from KwaZulu Natal and that small guy he is Sphesihle. She is his sister, that one over there, that small guy, yes that guy. He's smaller than me because he's one year younger. Let me show you now because then I am going to my other friend who lives across the road, up the road and then I have to cross it.

And look here, look at this money. You can't have the money, you can't take it, it's fake and I can't buy anything with it but I like it. I like to pretend that I am a big man, a rich man and so I like to show it to my friends. I never give it to them. I don't even let them hold it, but you can, you won't steal it, I know you won't. Where is Nigeria? Is it another place in the world? My teacher says that I should, when I get into another class, the bigger class, learn geography, and then I will know if Nigeria is a real place, is it a real place? Is it far away? How far away?

My dad, he never visits, my mother says he is dead but I know she only says this because she does not want to tell me that he just left us, me and my mother, but I know he did. He didn't die when I was born. I think he is around
here somewhere.

Maybe he is Nigerian, I think that he is Nigerian, and he has really gone away to wherever Nigeria is, that's why I keep this fake money. I want to show it to him when he comes around one day that I am rich. And he will come, I know that he will. I just have to wait. And then he can take the money and spend it in Nigeria.

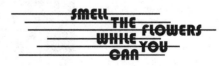

What is more beautiful
than a road?

I only have one story in my mind, a story of a tar road with potholes in it
and weary people walking down it. I have an image of a goat on the side
eating what is left of the garbage and everyone hating it all.

There are many stories
that make up a road.
Each person walks on
a different road and
meets up at a different
crossroad. But all
our roads are lost to
another; we never know
the other's road.

We should make a map of our lost roads.

Yes, a home on a road, a room on a road, an image of a room in a building on a busy road, this is a home, the building with a light outside, inside, waiting. This is a road.

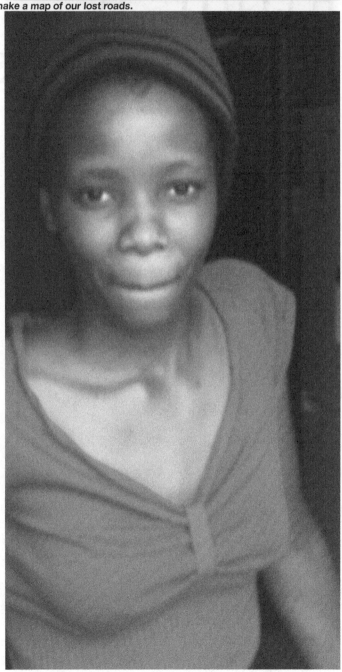

To: B
From: A
Re: Springs

I always think of dance as the art of movement, but also the art of the moment; it is ephemeral by nature, it leaves no trace, once a movement is executed it is gone, it is not rooted in permanence. A dance step, no matter that it is described in words that are always the same as the words that will be used to describe it again, it, the movement, is never the same, only the word is the same. Take the action of falling, this is a lead in ballet to a travelling step, the extended foot comes down to the floor with the leg bent, the weight of the body then shifts onto the front leg and the back leg lifts off the floor. Do you understand what I am describing here? This is maybe what I mean, the words are the same but the understanding is different, mine and yours. The dance step is the same, but the movement is different. And the choreographic methods that make the movements, they are also never the same. There is improvisation, the choreographer provides the dancers with a score that serves as guidelines for improvised movement. Like a score might direct one dancer to withdraw from another dancer, who in turn is directed to avoid the withdrawal or it might specify a sequence of movements that are to be executed but in an improvised way over the course of a musical phrase. So here the dance is never the same. But there is also planned choreography; here the choreographer dictates the motion and form in detail, leaving little or no opportunity for the dancer to exercise any personal interpretation. And yet even here the movement is never quite the same. We live a choreographed life, nothing much changes, and yet there is constant improvisation, as in dance, the words do not change, the movement does. I love my choreographed life, my habits. I think that if the habit is brief a person learns to love it, it is only enduring habits that chain one. And I think that a life without habit must be intolerable, I would hate to have to perpetually improvise. So I like the idea of planned choreography. Is it one of life's habits to endure? Is it one of life's habits to tell the same story over and over again? When you read my mails do you feel as if I have told you these stories before, once, a long time ago? I think that repetition is part of the story game, the game that we play, the game that children play. There is always a narrative ritual. The reader is never concerned with novelty, the story must always be told in the same words for even the slightest change will create some form of indignity as there is ritual and repetition in life. But my life, your life, is a happy life as while we exist in a repetitive mould, we are not confined, or are we? I seem to have written a lot in this mail. I don't want to read it, I just want to leave what I have said as is.

Do you live in perpetual anxiety; are you anxious that you will have no work today, anxious that one of your clients may not pay you, anxious that you will be violated in ways that you do not desire? Do you think that what you do is an abuse of power? Each thought, each action, a poison.

I live as if I live at the ocean; I am on the sea shore. The tide comes in and it goes out, and it comes in and it goes out, and some days something will be left behind, a valueless corroded silver coin, a sharp-edged broken bottle, a shell where the snail has died, a lifeless pink pattern of beauty; and other days there is nothing left on the sand but a shadow. I am at ease with what is not there as the tide recedes, and I am at ease with what it leaves behind. The ocean creates life and death, and when we die, we merely die, and when we live, we merely live.

So water is your life, and yet you do not live at the ocean. We are all dying it is true, ten years, ten thousand years, years of dying, ten years, ten thousand years, years of living. You are my girlfriend, can I understand you? Speak words, speak words that I understand, tell me what to believe for we do not live at the ocean, we live in Springs and it is surrounded by mine dumps.

Sex is like the water in the ocean, sometimes the waves are big, other times they are small and slow and lazy; sometimes they move in and sometimes they move out. But always something is there, something on the sand, a footprint, a shell, a sandcastle, a shadow. The memory of our sex is what is left on the sand, the smell of our sex makes me live, and the proof of this is that it always dies, washed away by the tides.

Madame Me you have a wolf, he laughs with white teeth, Madame Me you have two wolves; they laugh in your white shirt and bare their teeth at you. I snarl and shriek and growl.

Some Asian men put pearls in the foreskin of their penises to make it longer and wider, do you?

Maybe, listen to the sounds in
the bar, the hum of voice and
music. I do not enjoy
these sounds.

Nature dislikes silence and this bar is a part of nature, it embodies
what is not a vacuum, nature hates the vacuum, listen to the
sound of voices, they murmur and they scream. They fill the
vacuum.

Can I visit you tonight? Will
you need to work, or do you
think that you will be finished
by 7 o'clock?

Of course you can visit me tonight. I will change the curtains
in the room so that the night is always there and the lights from
the streetlamp outside the room will touch your skin and make
a patch-work quilt on it, and then I will stroke each segment
separately. I enjoy your skin in the half-light; it is so smooth it
makes me weep. I weep waterless tears, did you know that? I will
undress you with my laughter and my wine. I will taste you with
my tongue and with my eyes; my heart will beat and beat, and your
heart will be loved because when you are absent I sleep in a grave.

There are always nights of
tears, and there are always
nights of no tears. And my
heart will flow over your skin
as you stroke mine and I will
be content with just an hour;
this hour at the ocean.

We shall never be the defeated, we have the perfect solitude
of the lost.

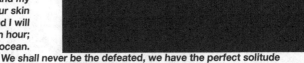

The Springs Hotel is painted a bright orange.

This is not the colour that it has always been; it was, many years ago, a modest pale cream. The concrete lines that put the orange in relief are now yellow, they are visible, contrasting. They reach upwards, vertically, in rows of four, and in between this are two rows of two.

In front of the hotel is a busy railway yard.

The short thin male receptionist stands behind the wooded counter, a built-in reception area. The edges of the wood are rounded, touched by many fingers, but on closer look the rounded pattern is carved into it. The receptionist wears a purple shirt with orange buttons sewn on it, you cannot see what trousers he wears for they are hidden by the reception counter.

No you cannot go upstairs, if you want to you must phone the manager, he is the owner, Carlos, here, this is his phone number.

The receptionist has a Nigerian accent, or at least I think that he has.

The door to the bar is a double door; there are two wooden panels, actually it is one door that looks like two. The panels are, as is the reception desk, curved and circular. At the level of your shoulder is a heart, round drops of blood drip from it, it is deeply carved into the dark panelled wood. The panels are fully open so that even if you are standing outside, just in front of the rounded reception desk, which you are, and if you look slightly to your right, without even bending forward, you can easily see inside the bar.

If you move slightly so that you are facing the door directly, or the double panels, squarely, you can see that on the what used to be white but now it is grey wall, set high, about three meters up, and directly in front of the door, on the opposite side of the room, is a television set. You cannot see what is showing from this distance, there is just a haze of colour and movement. You walk into the bar, closer, closer to the television set, or the end of the room, possibly just ten, or maybe five meters into the bar. Now you can see that the television is showing a pornographic film. At this time there is a man and a woman on the screen, the man is black and the woman is white, the man is penetrating the woman from behind. She is moaning. A clichéd image, it has been done time and time again and yet it is always an image that arouses.

Underneath the television screen sits a dark woman on a steel straight-backed chair. She has straight hair. There is a purple cushion with yellow lines on it behind her back; it seems to be stained with the smoke of many cigarettes. Her long hair reaches to her waist. It is black. If you look closely you notice a blonde streak in it, it reaches from the back to the front of her head, just to the right of her right eye. She is reading a book. You cannot see what it is for the cover is facing her lap. Then she looks up, and as she does so she holds the book up, the cover is now facing you. The title of the book is *Les 120 Journees de Sodome* by the Marquis de Sade. Her eyes are, blue, there are very few black women with blue eyes, somewhere in her lineage someone was raped by a white man, or a white man comforted her mother or her grandmother or her great-grandmother. Above her blue eyes the shadow is pink, and below them the liquid eye liner is black; she smiles a red smile, her lips do not move, they do not open. Her dress is green and reaches to below her knees, green with gold streaks; it looks as if a painter waved a wand at the material of this dress and covered it with gold, Jackson Pollock in Africa. It shines in the half light of the bar and flickers in the bright of the television. Her breasts are exposed; they are as small as tennis balls. Someone approaches her, a man dressed in a black suit and red tie, he does not look at her, he does not touch her, instead he leans over her and presses a button on the television set. She is not there.

The picture on the television screen changes, now there are two women on the screen. Both women, they are blonde and pale skinned, wear red dresses and red shoes. They lie on a bed talking to each other in what, if I strain my ears to listen, could be Russian, or at least an Eastern European language. A third woman enters the screen; she wears grey shorts and a backless shirt. She is also light skinned and blonde. She stops and looks at them for a moment. Then she leans down and lifts the corner of one red dress, she leans over the woman whose dress she has raised and begins to lick and suck. You turn away but can hear the screen moaning. You look up at it again, the other woman, the one who also wears the red dress, leans over to the table that is beside the bed, only now do you notice that on the table is a video camera. She presses a button. The

camera makes a whirring sound. Now there is another picture, another film.

On the wall, to the right of the television set, is a shelf. There are many empty glasses and half empty bottles of whisky and vodka and rum and cane spirits on the shelf. Just beneath the shelf is a notice: *Weekend special, R200 per hour for a room.*

From across the bar, slightly to the left if you turn to the right, a woman walks. She is upright, and then she stumbles, the yellow liquid that is in the glass in her hand slops onto the floor. You hear her speak, it could be a curse, but you are unable to hear it properly, or it may be that you do hear her but she speaks a language you cannot understand. She looks at you and then she turns away. On her purple dress, which is very short, so short that you can see that she wears no panties, there is a lot of blood. It must be blood for it is thick and viscous, it is not the thin liquid of red wine. She does not appear to have been damaged so possibly it is not her blood, it is someone else's.

As you walk slightly further into the room there is a wooden bar. It is long, a long bar. It stretches along the whole of the back wall. There are many filled ashtrays and empty glasses on it; occasionally you notice a glass that is half filled. The notice above the bar says: *Fish, all sorts for all sorts of prices - a sandwich for only R50.* The wood of the bar has patterns carved into it, rounded patterns; they curl around the grain of the wood. It is exceptionally ornate.

I am not sure that we will have lunch here. There does not seem to be too much on the menu.

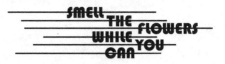

Today it is sultry in Springs, the air

around me is heavy, slugs that are trains move back and forth on the railway tracks, shunting, I can smell the sweat drip down from beneath my arms, the salt prickly, sticky. I walk into the bar of the Springs Hotel and wait; I am waiting for something, something to happen, someone, who?

There are many women around me, many women who slink and scowl and laugh. But I ignore them, for it is not they who I want to meet, I want to meet him, the man who holds the gun, the man who came here on most evenings, the man who shot it up, or did he?

A radio competes with the television for sound, I listen, it plays songs from the eighties, from a time before this change, they are retrospective sounds. A young twenty something bar-girl hums the note of a song that I recognise, she knows none of these words ... girls just wanna have fun ... oh oh yes ... girls just wanna have fun ...

Want something?

She winks, a wilting lid drawn down over a sun-soaked black eye.

I know why you are here; you want to look at all the people in this place. Everybody knows that you want to look at us; you say that you come to look at the building, this hotel, but we know that you want to look at us; you want to hear us speak. Why? Is it nice? is it sexy, why? Are we animals in a zoo?

She stands behind the bar counter, it surrounds the whole of the back wall of the room, the old wood is pitted and worn, but still the faint glow of polished walnut shows though the stains of many hands and many drinks that have been spilt in ecstasy of misery. She hands me a glass, it is as small as a tooth mug. In it is a brown liquid that is viscous and vicious. And as our fingers brush against each other I think of her voice, not her words, just the sound of the voice. It is a bitter voice but yet it is tinged with sweetness, like this bar, this building, bitter to have been something else, something venerated and on which white European hopes were painted, and sweet in that the something else has moved and it grows and is filled also with hopes, they are just different hopes.

Thanks, and I'll have another, and yes, I want to listen to you so tell me a story please, where are you from, what you are doing here, that kind of thing? I want to hear people

stories, not animal stories.

The girl's red mouth shakes as it laughs? Her round cheeks are shiny; she has no cheek bones, her make-up, a honey colour is too pale for her skin, it drips alongside her nose where the pores gape. There is a smear of lipstick on her upper left front tooth and her short-sleeved shirt is grim and green, it marks the crevices of her body, the curve of her stomach, rounded flesh. Her hand brushes against mine again as she hands me the glass. Her fingers are short, at their tips are long red nails, these are not piano playing fingers.

Came from a place about twenty kilometres away, it's a smaller town than this, two years ago, don't know, just came from there, suppose it was a place not far away, just up the road actually, and I wanted to be somewhere else. Then a guy here said I can have this job, he is from somewhere in Africa but he isn't black, he is more like an Arab but he speaks French, and I always wanted to make cocktails, but I don't make a lot in here, but I do get good tips. And I don't do what they do, those women, I don't have to because the manager looks after me. I like him, I think that I like Arabs, their religion is different to ours you know. He has a wife, but she doesn't live here, once he showed me a picture of her, she was covered up, I couldn't even see her face. It's mostly busy in the nights, then the people who live in these buildings that you look at come in, they do a lot of their business here, and also there are a lot of sales men are mostly just passing through, from Johannesburg you know.

She wipes her forehead with the back of her hand; the grease is caught up in her nails. She takes a towel from the bar counter and wipes it off.

I look up. On the ceiling and the wall in front of me are holes, bullet holes, the eyes of a warthog that once knew life gleam with the silver of death.

The girl notices me look up.

Another one?

A guy came in here one night and got into a fight, then he took the gun out and shot at the roof and at that wall, and at that pig, people were screaming and running, but he was not really trying to kill anyone, he was just showing off, showing that he had a gun and that he could use it. He couldn't speak

English, some foreign language, not a South Africa one, and not French like the manager, someone said he was from Bulgaria, but I don't know where that is, do you? Anyway it was in the newspaper. They came to take photographs, I was in one of the pictures, they printed it and I told them what happened. I was scared, the guy just took out his gun, then he shot, then he left. The police never found him; I don't know why because I told them where he lives, he lives in the building opposite, there, Regal House, it's a nice building inside, painted red. He still lives there, but he never comes here anymore, maybe he knows that the manager will kill him. I've still got my picture somewhere, the newspaper, they gave it to me; want me to find it for you?

No, it's okay, just tell me more stories.

I can't talk to you too much; I'll get into trouble, just for a little bit longer. I have a gun, the Arab manager he gave it to me, it's for protection you know, it's dangerous here, wild. She puts her hand underneath the bar and takes out a revolver; it has a short, blunt nose. She curls her forefinger around the barrel and puts it in her mouth. I'm not scared of guns.

Click.

And he shot at that pig, that one there on the wall that someone hunted before I came here, I think that pig was put on the wall a long time ago, there are no pigs in Springs now, not even outside on the farms. He shot it and shot it. And then he came over and wiped his fingers on my skirt. The other guys in the bar were cheering, and the pig, well it has dead glass eyes anyway, it can't feel or smell anything,
it's stuffed.

Look, there he is, he won't come in here, but there he is often in the street, the guy that shot this place.

She points to the road outside. A man walks past the window, past the front door of the hotel.

He is thin. I invent his eyes; they are dark blue with a cruel slyness in them. His gait is uneven. He walks slowly as if he is a cripple. I imagine that I know the face; it has delicate features and is unbearably sad, calm, cold blue eyes, an unimpeachable expression, lips that never smile. I lean forward and carefully, so that he is unaware of it, take a photograph for I want to know him, to know how he will always stare, look past me, focus on something outside me for I will never know him and his story. He is now a photograph and some words, my words, the girl's words, a taciturn man, he could be a seedy pederast, a vagabond trader, a vicious drug dealer?

Photographs are lonely, no-one inhabits them. They have no smell. They do not breathe. Will the words, my words, breathe into them?

And then he walks away and as he does so he turns his head towards the bar, he looks in my direction. He seems to look at me but I do not know if he sees me sitting here and staring from the window. And then he smiles, it is an acrimonious smile, and then he waves. He lifts up his right hand and waves. Is he waving at me? He raises his right hand and salutes the sun. And then he is gone.

I like the way he salutes the sun, it makes him appear as if he knows a god. Is he a god who waves to his god friends?

Thank you. I turn to the bar-girl, good-bye.

As I walk away I hear her hum the tune, ... girls just wanna have fun ... oh oh yes ... girls just wanna have fun ...

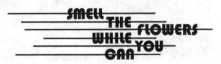

The medicine shop is on the ground floor

of Marie Court. Angela stands behind the wooden counter that is at the back of the shop. Alongside the walls are many shelves. On the shelves are roots and sticks and leaves and flowers and animal skin and stones and bones and hooves and the stain of old blood. The shop is dark. There is no light to hide the smell.

Hi, yes I know you; you came here last week with that young girl and the Chinese guy. What are you doing here? Oh, you want to look at the buildings, wait, I will call Zach, he is the caretaker of this one, no, not that one, there is another woman there, a white woman; I think her name is Debbie, but Zach can tell you some more. He has been here a long time, he says that he knows the owner because he was here as a young boy and his mother worked for the owner.

Behind Angela is a doorway which leads into the main hallway of the building.

On the projecting balconies of the building are children's toys and bicycles and lines of white washed clothes.

Yes I live here, and I also work here. I live in the flats upstairs, they are not that big but they are cheap. I will show you the flat that I live in if you want me to. I live with Abdul and my younger brother, he is my son, my blood, he came with me when I came down here from Uganda. I lived near to the Congo border, near to the Semliki River, there were a lot of mosquitos there. And the hot springs, the famous male and female hot springs are there, we take tourists there often. You can boil an egg in the water of the springs as they are so hot.

Wait here, I will call Zach, he is the caretaker, he can take you upstairs if you want to go there. I must not leave this shop because I am the only one who knows about the medicine that is here. I know it from Uganda, where I used to live.

Angela stands half inside and half outside the doorway of the hut.

The hut is bigger than a one roomed hut, the one roomed hut where the initiates live for six weeks, alone, where the door is always closed and there is no movement of the air. This hut, where she stands, is bigger. It has three rooms and is built to house the young women of the clan who may, or may not, be selected as initiates. These young women stay, and play, together. They must show that

they are responsible, that they are able to take on the strength of a healer, they must prove themselves able.

I have not been selected. Do I want to be selected? Or do I just want Abdul? And do I want him as he has been selected and to be the wife of a healer is powerful? Or do I want him as his skin is so smooth and when he penetrates me I can feel him, really feel him?

Angela does not stand upright; she slouches, against the doorframe.

An initiate does not slouch. My chances of being selected are not strong, but it is hard to stand upright always.

Abdul is not a Muslim, but he has taken the name Abdul for his father's brother, who came back from Kampala only a year ago, liked this name. And his father's brother is powerful, he can decide in the family who is named and what they are named. Abdul likes his name. It is a holy name. And Abdul, the son of a powerful man, has been selected as an initiate.

Angela watches Abdul. He holds the goat by its horns, or a horn, for she notices that it only has one horn, the other must have been removed, or it was lost in an accident. He holds the horn to his chest. His chest is naked; he wears only a piece of skin that is beaded around his waist, the horn cleaves into his hairless skin. Angela watches him. Abdul lets go of the horn, the goat drops to the ground. He takes a rope and ties it around the goat's neck. The goat is white with a few black markings, on its left front hoof there is a silver star. The rope, also white, blends into the goat skin so that no-one notices that it is not free.

Just now I know that Abdul must cut the throat of this goat. He will not cover me with blood, he must cover himself, he must take his tongue and lick it from his fingers, taste the warm life that becomes cold. I want this blood to cover me, to cover my skin. Then Abdul will touch me.

Abdul's father, the brother of his father, for a man has many fathers, walks up to the hut where Angela stands in the doorway. His skin is wrinkled; it hangs across his body and dresses him as a garment would, pleats.

Come outside, you must watch this. Abdul, he is getting ready for the ceremony. If you can watch this to the end it will help you to be selected. We want only strong women to be healers. Come outside, come, the sun is not

going to burn your light skin. The sun, it will burn only those who are not chosen, so think, think that it will not burn you. Think that you will be the chosen.

When will my turn come?

When you have practised the dance near to the hot springs, when the hot waters have burnt your skin, when you are strong enough to hold the goat to the ground and cut its throat. Come, come outside, this is how you will become strong.

But I have knowledge, knowledge of the medicine that we use.

You must let the sun warm, no, you must let it burn, before you can do the dance.

Wait, no just wait a little longer, Zach, he will come and talk to you; he can take you upstairs.

And now this white woman will ask about African medicine, and I must tell her. They always ask the same questions and I, I will always give the same answers. One day I will write it down and just give out the piece of paper to read then I don't have to tell them the same story over and over again.

Great, yes, I will wait for him. So tell me more about the medicine that you sell here? I don't know much about traditional medicine. If you have time while we wait for Zach can you tell me, I really would like to know more?

And here it is; the same questions.

Medicine, we keep all sorts of medicine. Mostly for the common kind of sicknesses that people suffer from, you know upset stomachs and headaches, but we also keep stuff for the serious ones, like AIDS, there is a lot of AIDS in my country, and here. Not AIDS cures, we do not have AIDS cures, no-one can cure AIDS, but we can cure all those things that go with it, like mouth sores.

Is this enough? I think I must say more. White people always think traditional healers kill and mutilate people and do things with body parts.

Muti is always thought to be used for witchcraft, medicine men taking body parts, killing. I think that this sometimes happens but not a lot, it is done by mad people who have evil thoughts. We use plants and animal things to cure. All of nature can be used as medicines, even poisons. Animals, yes sometimes they have to die to obtain the medicine.

White paper with faded black writing is stuck to the sides of the shelves, in some places is peeling off. The writing seems as if it was typed onto this paper a long time ago, the letters are formed by a typewriter.

Ubulawu, popoma, silene pilosellifolia makes you vomit, open the mind to dreams.

Rubia cordifolia cleans the liver and destroy tumours in the body.

Uzara Xysmalobium undulatum cures diarrhea.

Maphipa bark fixes acid in the stomach.

There, look, I have written some names on that paper. She will not understand. I must read the names to her; repeat them, so that she can remember.

I have a problem with my hip. I suffer from a sort of arthritis, do you have anything that may be of help?

Well yes, I have. There are a lot of problems with arthritis, especially because lots of people are injured often, injured in different ways, maybe they are stabbed or they fall down or something. Look here, take these herbs, eat them, every day before you have breakfast or before you take something in the morning.

A man walks into the shop, he steps from a doorway and stands behind Angela.

Abdul, this is Abdul, he works with me and he also knows about arthritis, his mother suffers from it. And sometimes so does Abdul. He was injured once by dancing too much. He was chosen.

Angela washes Abdul. Washes him, and she watches him.

I washed him when he was sick, after he ate the yellow dyed roots that the Batwa woman brought. I washed him when the blood of the goat that he killed filled all the crevices on his body; animal blood is not clean. I washed him when he was injured in the dance that was angry and furious, when his head smashed the red dirt floor. I washed him when he wanted my hands to touch him, the touch of me, living, not the touch of the ancestors, not the touch of the old women of the village who take it in turns to nurture him but who will never satisfy him.

The drums begin. Angela does not move. She does not want to come out from the doorway. She keeps herself inside her space; this is the place that she knows. She watches.

The drum, Abdul takes the red cloth from the woman who is his grandmother, the grandmother of the clan. He puts the cloth around his shoulders, then he takes the tail of the cow from her and winds it around his neck, then he places the animal skin over his shoulders. The drums continue, the women gather around him, he begins to scream and bangs his head against the ground, the sand is dense, there has been no rain, when he lifts his head from the sand Angela notices that

there is a red mark on his forehead.

I am a Christian. Hail Mary full of grace, blessed art thou among women and blessed is the fruit of thy womb, Jesus. Holy Mary, mother of God, pray for us sinners now and at the hour of our death. Does Abdul sin? Is the priest more beautiful in his purple robes? Is the mark, the red mark on Abdul's forehead, the mark of Cain? Cain, the man who tilled the soil and murdered his brother Abel because God favoured his brother, his brother who gave God animals in sacrifice not grains? But Abdul gives an animal to God, to the ancestors; he gives the goat, why is he marked as Cain was marked? No man will kill Abdul, this is his mark, his mark of Cain. But will he kill now that he has been called to the ancestors? Hail Mary full of grace, blessed art thou among women and blessed is the fruit of thy womb, Jesus. Holy Mary, mother of God, pray for us sinners now and at the hour of our death.

We are called. We are called. We are calling.

Angela follows the procession to the Sempaya hot springs, the sacred springs where eggs are boiled in the water and the ancestors are satiated with meat. Abdul lingers behind the women, the older women who call him. He lingers and watches Angela.

What is the story of these springs? Tell me again, tell me again?

When the women went to fetch firewood from the forest they saw a hairy man dressed in bark cloth, he carried a spear and a dog walked beside him. The women ran back to the village to tell the men of what they had seen. The men ran into the forest and found the hairy man, they brought him to the village but they did not kill him, they were afraid so they found him a wife instead. One day the man and the dog left the village. He never returned. After three days the men went out to search for him. At the hot spring they found a spear, and so this hot spring is called the male hot spring. The hairy man's wife was unhappy so she too ran to the forest, and she too never returned. Her clothes were found at a hot spring, and so it is called the female hot spring.

Abdul has been called by the ancestors. His mother left the village and began a relationship with her sister's best friend. She went to live in Kampala. And so, to make sure that the family is not disgraced, a son must be holy, the ancestors must support and nurture the family that has been betrayed.

Angela is not called by the ancestors. She sometimes wears the red robes and the lion skin. Abdul shares his auspicious clothing with her, but only in the dark.

Abdul leans over and beats the ground around the male spring. He is sweating, or is it that the hot water of the spring as it bursts from the ground soaks him. A woman, the grandmother's mother, hands him a calabash, it is filled with viscous liquid that is the red blood of the white and black goat mixed in with milk that is soured.

The liquid falls around Abdul's mouth, he licks it with his red tongue, his teeth are coloured by the juice of khat leaves. He is euphoric. Then he is led away, away from Angela and her eyes. She follows him.

The heat rises from the springs; there is steam in the air. The women go first to the female spring. A small hairy man rushes forward then he disappears into the steam. No one notices him; he is an ancestor, a ghost. Abdul walks towards the male spring. He lies down in the hot mud and screams for the steam that rises burns him. His voice comes from the steam; it joins with the figure of the small man. Angela watches Abdul. He lies still. The women beat him around his shoulders, then his thighs. He covers his head. The small man smiles as the woman call and sing. It is a funeral sound. And Abdul cannot catch him.

Is this a funeral, Abdul's funeral, the funeral of the death of a faith and the birth of another, the birth of the ancestors who are already dead?

Oh here he comes; here is Zach, the caretaker. Yes, he will show you the building. But come later, when I close the shop, and I will take you and show you the flat that I live in.

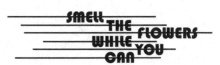

Debs is thirty-five years old, but she looks as if

she is forty-five for her hair is thin and lifeless, her pale pink skin is wrinkled and her fringe is stained yellow with nicotine. Debs smokes a lot, forty cigarettes a day. The lines around her eyes are fine and textured.

Debs lives in a studio flat on the fourth floor of Josette Towers. The building is owned by an Italian steel magnate who once owned many buildings in this street. Now he has sold most of them for the street is not what it once was; now it is not well maintained and different people live here, there are a few Europeans, some Asians and many Nigerians, and many of these are drug merchants. The steel magnate, it is rumoured, is not opposed to crime, who can be rich in times like these if opposed to crime, he is not opposed to these merchants, he is merely opposed to the street being dirty and the pavements crowded, and he is opposed to the depreciation of his assets. He was once, it is said and who can tell if this is true, involved with the Casa Nostra, a Sicilian Mafia family who wanted to establish a blood diamond route from Zimbabwe to South Africa. Are all Italians Mafiosi? No, he is Italian, so no stranger to crime (it is alleged). He is also the developer, or one of them, of the Springs Mall. This mall was built outside the town in what is perceived to be a safer area; few Nigerians live there and they have only had one cash-in-transit heist outside its main entrance, no one was killed, and there have been very few armed robberies, this may be because a local security company that is known for its no-nonsense approach patrols both inside and outside the mall all the twenty four hours of the day.

Debs has not lived here for a long time, although she was born and brought up in Springs and has lived in this town all her life. She likes to say that once she knew Nadine Gordimer, but this is not true, she never did know her, never even met her, although she does know which convent the Nobel Prize-winning author attended and directs people there. Debs is too young to have known Nadine Gordimer for she left Springs many years ago, Debs does not know that Nadine Gordimer was Jewish, and Debs is not keen on Jews, and she may not even have been born when Nadine Gordimer lived in Springs, but Debs does not know this and so she continues to tell people that she knew her, not well, but she did know her. They had a

coffee now and again. And she has read all of her novels, or at least read about them. She knows a lot about the first novel, *The Lying Days*, for this was about Springs, life in a mining town. Debs's father was a mine manager, as was Nadine's. Debs believes that they have a shared history, they have a bond.

Josette Towers was, in what Debs's mother always said, built in 'the good old days' and was sought-after accommodation for the residents of Springs, the only unfortunate part of this, in Debs's mother's view, was that many Jews lived in the town and many lived in the building. Often Debs's mother, well not any more for she is dead, she died three years ago of lung cancer, they tried to save her with chemotherapy but, as Debs says, the doctors didn't care, they just wanted to make more money, and it was the chemotherapy that killed her. She would have died anyway, after all she did have lung cancer, Debs knows this, but she also knows that she would not have died in such an undignified way. Anyway when she was alive she would always discuss the 'good old days' with Debs. The days where there were very few black people in the streets of Springs, although there were Jews, and certainly no black people lived in the buildings, or the building where Debs now lives and where her mother, for a few years, also did. Debs still sleeps in the bed that her mother died in; she believes that this keeps her memory alive.

Debs does not mind that black people live in the building, she minds them less than she minds Jews, at least you can recognize a black person, they are, the black people, very friendly. Often she is asked around for a cup of tea, or something stronger, and it is the stronger that Debs likes, she likes this a lot. There are many children in the building. Debs has no children, and will probably not have them as she does not believe that it is a woman's duty to breed, as her mother believed, and she will never, even though she enjoys the company of her neighbours, adopt a black child. The reason for this, she thinks, is that it would be difficult, for the child that is, to have to experience such vast cultural differences, but also, while not admitting this, she does not want to share her space with a black child, he, or she, could easily become a thief or a murderer, or even a terrorist. And of

course there is Sanette, who she likes to meet in the mornings and fuck, and of course, the whisky which she drinks, but only after ten.

Debs likes staying in Springs. She enjoys the vibrancy of the streets and she enjoys hearing everyone, white people that is, say to her 'how can you live in an area with all those blacks and the drug addicts and the prostitutes'? They admire her. And she enjoys it that the black people around respect her, she thinks that they respect her, because she lives with them, in fact she lives so close to them that she can often hear the sounds in the flat next door. The walls of the building are not thin but many flats have been divided with dry walling so they have in them paper-thin wooden walls. She divided her mother's flat into two parts because she can get more money if she rents out the one half. And Debs needs the cash, being a caretaker does not pay much and she likes to buy whisky, sometimes gin, and Sanette is expensive, not expensive in that she is a whore like the whores that work at the Springs hotel, but she does have needs, like leather jackets and expensive jeans and striped shirts. Sanette is married and wants to be divorced but she can't afford to be, so she stays married and fucks her husband, Koort, often. Koort does not know this but Sanette want to become a man, or as she likes to say for she has read that this is the way it is said, transition from woman to man as she was born in the wrong body. But to transition is expensive even though hormones are more easily available than they were in the past, and Debs knows that she can get them from Hoppies Chemist, the only chemist in the town, they order them especially for her. Debs likes Sanette, she often says that she loves her, or him, and so she contributes to this transition by paying for the hormones for both she and Sanette know that Koort will definitely not do so.

Debs likes it when people come to the building, and they don't do this that often. She likes to show her knowledge of the Art Deco architectural style, she knows about the curves and the portholes and that the buildings were often designed to look like ships even though Josette Towers does not look like a ship, but despite the drab grey paint it is easy to see the elongated roundness of the windows and the way the cornices are made to look like wings. She enjoys taking people inside her flat to show them the flower-shaped brass taps in the bathroom, and how the brass window clasps are beaten into the shape of roses.

Debs likes living in Josette Towers. It offers her a life that the 'good old days' never could.

It offers her freedom.

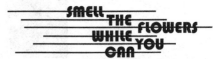

We can't just go off
without knowing where
we are going to.
Why not?
Well for a start we need
to take enough money
to pay the tolls at the
toll booths.

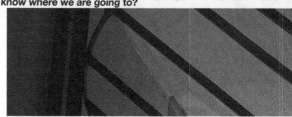

Do we ever know where we are going to?
I have been to Springs,
but I don't really know
it, in fact I don't know it
at all, it is just there, a
place that I have been
to sometime, once long
ago. I think you have to
take the highway, the
R77, to the East Rand.

I did not know that Springs has a whole lot of the Art Deco Buildings.
So what are you
saying?

We need to get a map, or we need to get a guide.
What is a map except
that which the map
maker wants us to read,
we can just ask people.

People say what they want us to hear, they paint a picture of themselves
that they want us to believe, that they believe, but what do they not
say that they do not want us to hear? It is the same with maps, the map
maker draws a map of the place that only he can describe, the story of
the map is his story.
Maps do not tell us the
stories of those that
walk on its lines.
Neither does a guide.
We must write the
stories of those who
walked on its lines.
We must become the guide.

A map maker in a great empire created a map that was so detailed it was as large as the empire itself. The map was expanded and destroyed as the empire conquered or lost territory. When the empire crumbled, all that was left was the map.

Yes, now pass me the map, the Springs map?

To: B
From: A
Re: Springs

Hey, hello, how are you doing up there in New York City? I say up there because if I look at a map, and I have been doing this lately, the United States is always at the top of the page, the whole American continent is always at the top of the page. Anyway you came to mind as I was looking at a map of the world, an atlas actually, and when I opened a page, at random, there it was, the land of the free and the home of the brave, the United States of America, the East Coast, and New York City plumb there in the middle. Are you brave, are you free? You once were, as I think, was I? But it got me thinking of you and maps, and the idea of maps and the movement of maps and the movement of those who follow maps. So I went to the Ekurhuleni Town Council and looked for old maps of Springs. Anyway the guy there that worked in the archives section didn't know much about Springs, he said that he was from Pretoria and had been transferred to Ekurhuleni, but he was learning about the area. He told me that in addition to the most famous Charlize Theron, the less famous Grace Mugabe, I think she is very famous, and James Phillips, who I am not sure that many people know of, were born on the East Rand; Grace in Benoni and James in Springs. He told me that the council in Pretoria was retrenching people, or something, and so he took a transfer instead of being fired, and ended up here, says he likes living here; it's a bit like living in another era. He let me into the archive and we did find some of the old maps. Not as interesting as I thought but it did get me thinking. The first map that I looked at showed the first Springs, or the first drawing of Springs on a map, it described the boundaries and detailed the territory of, as it was called then, The Springs. And then as The Springs began to move and to change into Springs, so the map was expanded, the old map was destroyed and replaced, and the new one was detailed differently. And then I looked at another map, a more recent one, and I thought that I don't live here, this place that is in the map, and yet the people of Springs do live in the map, and every day, when they look at the map, they must make sure that their place in the town is properly described and detailed; detailed and described by the map-makers, like I want them to do, like I want to make sure happens. I want them to describe my Springs, put in my details. But the map-makers no longer know what to name the streets or on which longitude they lie or who lives here. And so the map is crumbling away from over-use or dis-use, and where does that leave the place where I live? But, and I think that I may do this, I will write the map, I will draw the map, the map will tell the story of my Springs, my movement in the town, the movement of the people as I perceive them, as I identify them. And so I did a quick coupé jeté en tournant, it's a ballet term for really just moving in a circle, a compound, or lots of steps, done in a circle, so you change the foot that supports you all the time as you move and create the circle. I did this because I wanted to make a map and so complete a 360-degree turn using different feet to do this. I want to make a map in which the tail of the snake enters its own mouth, I want to make a Mobius strip, the movement of the town has just changed but the streets and the roads and the buildings are still the same, and the people are changed but they are still the same. And so I can complete the circle.

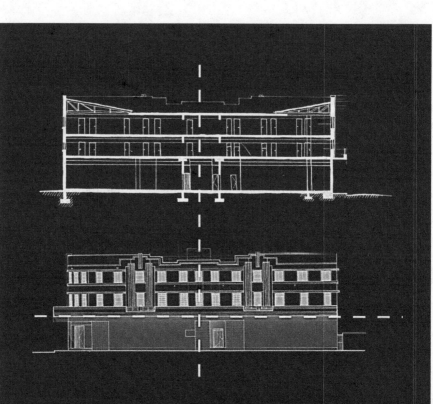

[crenellations – regularly spaced teeth-like projections on the top of a wall, originally derived from defence-like structures, but now used as decoration in most art deco buildings]

Dr Lungile: There is no problem without a solution:
are you feeling down. can't think what to do next.
well waiting no longer. give us a call now and free
yourself from all your problems.
We are gifted with special powers that allow them
to see through the future and the past. and able to
solve all kinds of problems.
Find Dr Lungile in the town. Call for an appoint-
ment and directions.
/Lost Lovers
/Magic Ring
/House Cleaning
/Sexual Problems
/Business Problems
/Promotion at Work
CALL: +27 63 256 7004

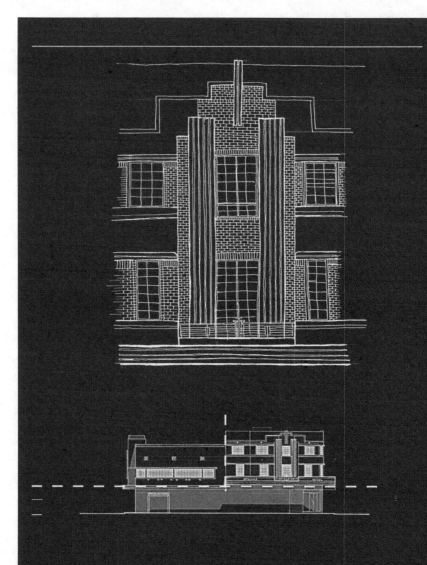

[sanctuary – the high altar in a church is situated in the sanctuary, it is the most sacred part of the church; if the church is built in the form of the cross the sanctuary is at its head]

An American in Africa (Africa is one country) says:

The coolest Art Deco building in Springs is the Central Fire Station. I got there too late and missed the lesson about the fire station, unfortunately. But it doesn't take an expert to figure out that this is the coolest fire station in the world. Art Deco, it's a very cool idea, these Cubists and Surrealists and Futurists were very cool, awesome, sick man.

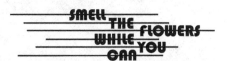

THIS STONE W

BY

HIS WORSHIP T

CR. GEO. J

J.P. M.P

ON DEC 1ST

The Springs Fire Station is a yellow building;

and the walls, some of them are beige. As you face the front of the building, if you are standing across the street from the fire station, or if you are standing on the same side of the street, although on the same side you do not get a panoramic vista of the building, you will notice a mixture of the square and the round. On either side of the building the walls are rounded, as are the openings into it, whereas in the middle it is square. There are four fire truck doors; they are all made of a dark brown wood. If you walk over to them and look closely you will notice the heavy metal hinges, they keep the doors closed. The doors have been recently restored, a drunken traveller smashed into them one Saturday night, but now they are repaired. But the doors no longer allow the fire trucks through, modern trucks are built to be bigger and better than those that were built one hundred years ago, and so the doors do not allow access to these modern engines. They are always closed. Closed and restored, used; sullied.

All along the walls of the building are portholes, windows in a ship. The curved lines dwell in your mind long after you leave this building, the curved staircases on either side of the inside of the building, the poles that lean down and on which the firemen dance whenever a fire bell rings. The façade is stairs and stars; dimension and rhythm, a leap (of faith). The fine painted crest says power and lineage and gets polished twice a week (in colours as fresh as the day the ribbon was cut) and the sign over the door says *Carpe Diem*. The fire station is guarded by fire-breathing dragons, dragons are imaginative creatures, much like unicorns; fires fire mystery, they burn down dreams but the stars too are fire.

Scream scream scream into the dying flames of the night, ships and aircraft and wheels .....

Springs Fire Station was designed by Mr Freddie Anifantakis. He lives at 241770 Street, Agios Dimitrios 71202, Heraklion. Heraklion, Greece.

Or is this someone else?

Mr du Plessis is a fireman; he has been a fireman for twenty years. He is tall and big and has all his hair.

Mr Botha is also a fireman; he has been a fireman for twenty-eight years. He is short

and stout and has very little hair.

Mr du Plessis believes that to be a fireman is an honour; it is a passion, a calling.

I am honoured to be a fireman, as am I honoured to work in this building, this piece of heritage, and our heritage is dying, burning up, disintegrating. But I am honoured. Did you know that not everyone can be a fireman? It takes a special calling. It is like the calling to Christ, to our Lord, and I, I was a pastor before I was a fireman. I was a pastor in the Springs Fire station. In those days they knew that Christ must be in our hearts. I have Christ in my heart, do you?

Mr du Plessis, when he was the pastor, counselled the bereaved, the lonely, the heartbroken, this too was a calling, an imperative calling, the bereaved and the lonely and the heartbroken need to be mended, and only a pastor who knows how to fight fires can mend them. Christ fixes them up fast.

Now Mr du Plessis is not a pastor at the fire station, there is no pastor at the fire station, a pastor is never called on to perform pastoral duties. And so he is merely a fireman.

I started out as a rookie, then I became a junior fireman, then a fireman officer then a senior fireman and all the while I never received the same salary as when I was a pastor. Christ rewards those who believe, maybe I should have stayed a pastor and not become a fireman, but then I would have no job, no better it is that I am fireman because now I am a senior fireman.

There are a lot of fires in Springs.

It is always in the overcrowded flats, it's because they overuse the electricity, overload it, and always there are so many people in one flat. They are poor, and they don't have houses. And of course we go out to the squatter camps, what are the better words, informal settlements, and then the fires are started because there are a lot of illegal electricity connections and they also light a lot of fires which then get out of control.

We go out a lot and always there are dead people. Dead people can't talk or tell you what happened so most of the time I have nothing to say, like those dead people, sometimes I feel dead, when I look into the eye of a dead man I sometimes wonder if this is what my eyes look like, dead. Many children get caught in the fires, it's because the parents

are drunk; alcohol, it's a bad thing, bad, very bad. I drink, I drink to forget, brandy and coke is a very good drink, it's sweet. You can't believe what a dead child looks like, not very nice, not very nice at all. He just lies still, he does not move, except sometimes the hands move. A doctor told me that when a person gets burnt the nerves are not killed, but they will soon die because there is no oxygen in the blood. And so the hands move when the body is burnt completely. The dead children, they are always in my dreams.

I imagine that there is
nothing funnier than
unhappiness.
It is surely the most comical thing in the world.

**We laugh,
we always laugh
in the beginning.**

*Yes, unhappiness, it's like a funny story that is heard too often,
we find it funny but now we don't laugh anymore.*

To: B
From: A
Re: Springs

Hey hello again. I like it, this communication, technology brings us closer even though we are far away from each other. I like to dance. Did you know that a jeté is a leap in which one leg appears to be thrown in the direction of the movement? So the dancer leaps forward while at the same time he throws his leg forward. I am thinking of this as sometime soon I have to prepare a lecture on the housing crisis in Johannesburg, actually the East Rand, and all I am doing is reading about the Art Deco buildings that are here. In fact, because I live here and can get to them pretty easily, I often go and take a look at some of them. They are all in one street really so I can just walk down the street and look. I romanticise buildings, maybe I romanticise architecture, the idea that someone is able to create three-dimensional art. I want to own an Art Deco building in Springs, there I go again, ownership, I romanticise ownership, and so, well then if I romanticise ownership and want to own property, specifically an Art Deco building, then I need the money. So wow, I can now say that I am imaginative about money, I am investing, or I fantasise that I am investing in art, property art. Did you know that there are several kinds of jetés? I am doing one as I hurry along the road to happiness, or unhappiness, much the same thing, it is just the un that is different. And as I hurry along this road I imagine that I am a clown, for happiness is a clownish condition, and sometimes I imagine that I am a ballet dancer as I am a witness in this movement of time, this movement of ideas, this movement of a town, these dance steps of change. You didn't know me when I was a child, but I was, or I thought I was, for a short while, going to be a ballet dancer. Then I didn't become one, I fell and broke my ankle so it was too weak to hold my body. But I know about ballet. A grand jeté is a very big jump, it is initiated from bent legs. It resembles the splits in the air. It is as if, when I walk down 3rd Avenue, that I am split in half; in the one split I love the buildings and the sound of different languages and on the other hand I know it is dirty and I am afraid of what I do not know, afraid maybe of them and what they destroy, they, they are not me. And of course when I am thinking all of this movement of ideas stuff my ankle begins to hurt, badly. Sometimes I think that it is really crap that these buildings are being destroyed, the frontages covered in metal roll doors to prevent thieves getting in them, the flats divided into rooms with dry walling, the lifts that do not work, the windows smashed in, the metal work of the staircase balustrades stolen. And at other times I think it is amazing this mix of people and sound and colour. It really is a dance, the Rite of Spring maybe?

To: B
From: A
Re: Springs

Today I sat on the pavement outside the Pakistani shop, the one on 3rd Avenue, well you won't know where I am talking about as there a lot of Pakistani shops on this street, and you don't really know the street, and anyway even if you did even I am uncertain whether they are Pakistani or if they are Bangladeshi or Indian, and you know, they all look alike, they all speak with the same accent, or rather I should say that I am unable to discern any difference in accent. And then in front of me, well not directly in front, but rather slightly to my right. I did not have to turn my head to look, but I could look, and I could also see the people walking on the pavement opposite me, and there was a truck, a pink and green truck. The truck was filled with cabbages and a man, he was very dark and tall, possibly he was from the Sudan, you know how dark people in the Sudan are, Nubian, I have looked at that book by Leni Riefenstahl, you must know that book, she went out to the Sudan and took pictures of beautiful people, much like she took pictures of beautiful Germans except these were Sudanese and of course they were black, ebony in fact, rather than white and porcelain, I wonder if she asked them to polish their skin, oil it. Anyway this man, who I thought was Sudanese, he was taking the cabbages from the truck and packing them into a crate. Suddenly he began to move, a sort of jeté as he started from bent knees, as he jumped from his knees he transferred his weight to his standing legs, one leg actually, then he bent again into a plié, that ballet movement, and placed the foot of the other leg behind him. And all the while the green cabbages were being piled into the crate. And while he moved in this dance I saw an Orwellian spectacle, someone had crept in front of the truck and had taken a gun from under a long black coat, and suddenly this dancing Sudanese was filled with holes, and the pavement turned pink around him and the cabbages were a sickly green pink colour, like the edges of the rainbow where the green meets the red. And then suddenly the Sudanese man fell over, he really did fall over, dead. And a cabbage rolled off the pavement and into the road. Cars drove over the cabbages, they were squashed, like a bug, like when I notice one running on the kitchen counter and bang my hand on it, and the people who were walking by just laughed and laughed. Is the world a place of permanent war? Nothing changes, even in Springs people die, maybe you are right, all the world is a cemetery, the present is a fantasy of the past, or the past is a fantasy of the present.

Razias Halaal Foods: This is Nazeem's shop.

Nazeem has white hair. He is stocky and he stands upright, his hips and shoulders are lined up, he must be about fifty. He owns this shop; a takeaway food shop and, because he is Muslim, he sells no pork or alcohol even though people often ask him for it, and he would, should he sell it, make much more money than he does at the moment. On the outside of the shop there is a red and white sign, the words SPICY TAKEOUTS – CHEAP are written on it in black letters. To get into the shop, which has two wide open doors, there is one step. From the pavement the shop looks like any other food shop in this main road, it could be run down and dirty. Inside the shop, after one has taken the one step, it is not dirty, the floors are swept and the counters gleam. Nazeem wears a white shirt, he stands behind the counter. Behind him, to his left, is a large kitchen, it extends far back into the building, so far that the back walls are not visible. Here there is movement; many people move about, they don't stop moving, cutting, chopping, boiling, oiling, cleaning.

Nazeem is always on the telephone.

Yes, can do; forty samosas, all chicken, and forty cheese ones, and the roti, half half, vegetable and beef, for sure. And cold drinks, have coke and lemonade and some Fanta, OK how many, yes, perfect, will get it delivered by 1 o'clock at the latest, no you want it earlier, OK will try, 12 then, we will have to work extra hard to get it all done by then, but it will be done, of course I will have to charge more, fine, you need it, OK.'

I live in Benoni and come here every day. It's not that far to drive here, but I stay there because Benoni is a much better place to live in, it is not as run down as Springs is, it is clean, better quality, and there are more people who have lived in this country for a long time there, you know what I mean. And a lot of Indians, we live near the lake, but here, in Springs, it is like an African city, everyone is a foreigner, you know that all African cities like Lagos and Nairobi, they are filled with foreigners. We are becoming like that. Everyone here is foreign. If you walk down the street you will see that all the shops are run by foreigners, some from Bangladesh, some Ethiopia, all over Africa, just talk to them and you will get the picture, some may not talk to you, they might be too scared because a lot of them are illegal, haven't got the work permit or residence permit that they need, it is hard to get a residence permit to live in this country, I know this, my brother's son wanted to marry a girl from Pakistan and they wouldn't give her the permit even though he said that he was South African and was going to marry her, so I don't know how these people get into the country, how they stay here. I am not saying anything, but the police, often they are here, talking to people, but no-one gets arrested, I don't know, I am not saying anything, but you know what I mean. There is so much corruption, like it is in all African cities. These people, they undercut us in business. Look at the next door shop, it is owned by a Pakistani, he has his family, at least I think it is his family there, two woman and four children, well adult children, maybe twenty or so, they all sell and help out, the wives and the others, and then he sends all the money he earns, maybe not all of it, but a lot, to the rest of his family in Pakistan. It is a cash business, no taxes, and he rents the shop and he lives there at the back, all of them live there so it is not so expensive for him. You should see the bathrooms behind these buildings, they are dirty because people live here, they don't have a flat or a house, they just live in the back of the shop and wash and use the bathrooms at the back. If you go into the shops, most of them and ask to go to the back they will never take you because then you will know that they live there, have a bed and a fridge and all of that stuff, even a primus stove. It is crowded at the back of these buildings. So it is no wonder that they can sell their stuff for such a cheap price, they don't have to pay rent for anything except the shop. So how can we compete? Even me, I will buy from them; it is cheaper, much cheaper. I don't know where they get their stuff from, maybe China, but it is so cheap. So even though I want to support South Africa and South Africans, and the South African shops, they are more expensive, these ones are very cheap. An African city, yes that is what this town is becoming, you know. And the malls don't help us either.

Have you been to the Springs Mall, you must go, it is new, beautiful, it is clean and has

the big shops in it; Mugg and Bean, Pick-n-
Pay, that kind of thing, people go shopping
at the mall, it is clean and everything is there,
they don't support the small shops anymore
not like they used to. Go to the Springs Mall,
it is beautiful, not dirty like this street, what a
beautiful place. But it does not help us in the
town, no, not at all. I own this building. I have
owned it for a long time, my father owned
it, well he didn't really, you know in the
apartheid times we Indians could not own
property, so he owned it in a company with
a white guy, now I own it, we don't need the
white owners anymore, so I just own it, bought
the white guy out, and my son will also own
it when I die. There are no rooms above it,
no flats, just the building; it goes across the
whole block. I make good money here. I
am known in the area as my food is good.
Yes, you like it, next time you come you must
phone before and I will make the samosas,
have the roti with vegetables, and then if you
want to I will give you the special, the roti
with chips, just R9.00 more, and you get the
whole lot, roti, vegetables and chips, cheap,
not expensive. Everyone, all my clients, love
the samosa and the roti, we make them all
here in the kitchen at the back. I have trained
all the staff, have the best Indian cooks even
though they are not Indian, but they are South
African, and one guy is a Zimbabwean, and
the other from Zambia. All the offices on the
East Rand come and buy food here for their
office functions and that kind of thing, they
don't come actually, they think that Springs is
dangerous, but they phone, they know me, I
am reliable and I deliver to them all the time.
    'Yes, I have them, but it will take a while as
we have to fry them up, not so long maybe
15 minutes, you will wait, then my driver will
come, maybe another 15 minutes, good, just
give him the money, R120.00, yes good.'

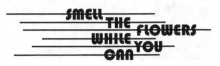

The building in 2nd Avenue is two stories high

is two storeys high. It is painted a bright turquoise, there are no signs that it has aged for the turquoise is smooth, it is unmarked. The signage on and above the blue wall is in red; above the three large open doors to the building is the word SOLLY'S, in capital letters, then to the left is a hanging sign, it does not look at the street but rather faces up the road towards a sign that says Olympic Club. Underneath the words Olympic Club is a picture of a naked woman who has long straight hair. The writing that faces this sign is orange set against a white background, it says Solly's Textiles. And then painted onto the walls are three signs in blue, blue lettering against a yellow background; the first says upholstery fabric and vinyl, upholstery sheets, the second says taxi flooring and carpets, motor car seats and fabric, and the third says haberdashery dress and church fabric.

At the entrance to the building, just before you step into the shop is a security guard, he does not hold a large machine gun, but if you look closely he has a bulge underneath his jacket, a hand gun, for he is there is guard the shop, and Solly?

Solly has a long beard. He wears a white skull cap as all Muslim men who are believers do. He sits behind the raised counter. Next to him, also behind the counter, is a young woman, she is not, or she does not appear to be Muslim, it seems that she is an employee.

But what are appearances, the eye deceives and stereotypes tell just one story.

Amazing, I have been looking for material like this for a while, you can't find this kind of tartan often, or if you do find it is made of thick wool, imported from Scotland where it is cold, and it is very expensive. This is fantastic, it is light, some cotton in it I think, but I love the tartan pattern. You know me, I am a name dropping fashion aficionado, so yesterday when I looked at the website for Vivienne Westwood I noticed these amazing tartan pants, and expensive, something like six hundred pounds, and I thought that if I can get material and make them, take them to the tailor that is down the road from where I live, I could get these pants made for far less than I could buy them from Vivienne Westwood, and who would know. I would never say anything, I would just look at people admiring them and speculating, where from Paris, New

York, London, never Springs. I don't have a problem with ersatz, and anyway you do know what is said about all that fake stuff that comes from Thailand and China? The factories are owned by the big designers, why wouldn't they want to control their own imitations, they know that it is going to happen so they control it. And this is amazing stuff. Look here, look at this red tartan and a brown one, which do you think I should buy. Both?

How much do you sell it for?

Seventy Rands a meter.

Gosh that is not expensive. What is it made from?

A little wool, but not a lot so you can wash it easily, nylon and a little cotton, this is good material; we sell a lot of it.

Yes I know that it is not wool, not like Vivienne's are, but we live in Johannesburg not London so I figure that I don't need wool because then I would only wear them in winter and even then how cold does it get here?

Vivienne would be proud to see what I am doing. You don't think so?

Hey I don't think that she is in it for the money, oh OK maybe she is now, but she was not always. She made clothes for Sid Vicious and Jonny Rotten, she was married to Malcolm McLaren, the guy who managed the Sex Pistols and her shop in the King's Road, I think it was called SEX, was the go to shop for all the London punks then. She was the doyenne of the punk era. So I think that she would like this subversion of the system. Subversion, that's the only resistance nowadays, even Vivienne is mainstream now.

But I don't have cash, and I think the sign at the door said no credit cards.

Good afternoon. Yes, I am Solly, the owner of this shop. Yes we do take credit cards, but you can't pay on a budget account. This is because I am a Muslim and I don't believe in interest so I won't have anyone purchase anything with interest. But I will take a credit card if you pay on straight, not budget.

I have owned this building for a long time; it has been in my family, my father owned it even though he did not, it was apartheid then. No there is no upstairs so you can't go up, there are some workmen on the roof but

you don't want to go up there, it is dangerous, they are fixing the tiles. Yes this shop, my shop, Solly's Textiles has been here for a long time, we do everything, dress material, tablecloths, curtains everything. And we are well known because we have been here a long time. People know this so even though they don't live in Springs anymore they still come through to buy the material. We have a lot of clients, they come from all over, even the taxi drivers come to buy for mini-buses and Christian women, they buy so that they can make dresses to wear to church. And my prices are cheap. I like this place, but I do not like the club that is next door to the shop, they drink alcohol there and often there is noise.

Thank you. I will take the tartans, both of them, the red and the brown, no, no zip, the waist will be elasticised. How much do I need, fine, 1, 25 metres, so how much does that make it, perfect? I will take it to a tailor and make the perfect Vivienne Westwood creation.

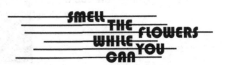

Remember when we bought
that material in the shop
in Springs?
Yes, for my fake trousers.
Well it got me thinking. What
about a fashion show here, here
in this place, there are all these
stunning buildings?

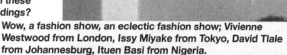

Wow, a fashion show, an eclectic fashion show; Vivienne
Westwood from London, Issy Miyake from Tokyo, David Tlale
from Johannesburg, Ituen Basi from Nigeria.
Well David Tlale is now
from New York.
And Ituen Basi is now from London.

Fantastic! This performance
will show up the beauty of the
decay, the magnificence of what
is and what can be, beauty is
truth, truth beauty, upmarket
fashion can tease the fiery
smoky spirit of Springs.
Mmm, yes, the consumption of clothes, the consumption of
buildings, beauty, that is all we need to know on earth, for where
does it all end, dust to dust, ashes to ashes, dust in the crevices
of the Miyake Pleats Please black trousers.
The buildings can be a
showcase for fabric and
fashion, in and on and outside,
the faded and electric glass
windows can frame a blue and
grey sequined shirt and the
multi coloured silk waistcoat
that reaches to the floor. This
design, this architecture calls
for an explosion of bright and
clashing tones, the Art Deco
decoration of clothes will walk
the corridor in Manitoba House,
walk the aisles at Shimwells,
floral and animal motifs in an
overcoat will glance through the
red curved porthole windows in
Regal House, hang on a laundry
line with faded rainbow white
sheets, pink velvet gloves will
caress the iron and wooden
balustrades of Renestra House
and a parrot in velvet and green
can talk to a child on the stairs
of Carlow Court.
It all goes very well together.

Yes, fashion is an ephemeral thing, here today and gone tomorrow, and Art Deco, it was here today gone tomorrow; no-one is content with the indispensable, the superfluous is always needed, the superficial is our depth for otherwise where is fashion and music, flowers, and perfumes, and where are these buildings. Camp! What about jewellery? Art Deco was famous for its jewellery designs.

Jewellery and clothing, we can find diamonds and surround them with colourful gemstones cut into the shape of leaves, fruit and flowers. We can combine jade and coral for clothes need jewellery; sleeveless dresses mean that arms need decoration, bracelets of gold and silver encrusted with lapis-lazuli, onyx and coral, and short hair needs Art Deco earrings, intricate geometric patterns of skyscrapers; pendants of fruit, flowers, frogs, fairies, mermaids made of sculpted glass that hang on cords of tasselled silk.

And the dresses, the capes, think of rectangular and triangular patterns embedded with pearls in lines on onyx.

Wow, the model is, will be, a highly polished Marinetti machine.

It will be a performance, a spirited fabulous contrary contradiction; a playful way of showing the buildings, the decay and the destruction and the fleeting, the evanescent exoticism of what is now another.

New conditions for new experiences, rebellion in the streets as our dead eyes follow and photograph, destabilise as tartan trousers and Vivienne Westwood, is toppled by cloth bought at Solly's Textiles.

To: B
From: A
Re: Springs

The longer I stay here the more I begin to think that this town is a gold mine although there is no more gold in it; all the mines have closed down. They closed in the early nineties when it began to be less profitable to mine in the area, so they just closed up and left. And they left a people behind, and then the people left too, left for, I suppose what they would call greener pastures, and now other people live here, new people who do not know what gold smells of. But it is a gold mine, for me anyway, yes, a gold mine. I can hear you saying to yourself as you read this, how, how can this be more than just a dump, another Detroit? And I, I imagine a theme park. There are so many amazing buildings in this town, the Springs Hotel, the Court Chambers, the most fantastic examples of this architecture. I haven't seen so many examples of this type of design since I looked at photographs of Miami, yes, America. Miami, it has a lot more of this kind of building in it, of course it has a lot more, it is in America. Sometimes I dream of being an American, do you? And then I think that yes I can be one; you can be one here, in this town, in Springs. If a man works hard and makes his way to the top of the mountain (he can even make his way into the White House), dreams can come true. They can, in America, it is the land of the dream, and here, I can also make these dreams come true, create hopes and desires and fantasies. A small cat walks on the balcony next door. It is orange and has a white face. From where I stand I can see that it, maybe it is he, has long hair. I think that if he were to rub against velvet trousers he would leave his mark behind, his orange hair. He makes me think of that movement of the cat, the pas de chat is the step of the cat, or the jump of the cat. The small orange cat jumps to catch an insect, possibly a moth, the pas de chat is a travelling sideways jump where while in mid-air the legs are bent, with the feet as high up as possible and the knees apart. In Russia the cats are different; there the cat jumps a jump where the legs are thrust out backwards not forwards. I watch the small orange cat jump, I can't tell if he is Russian or not. But why was I writing about cats and movement, maybe because I am watching this small orange cat, maybe because I can feel how the town could move, backwards and forwards and jump, if it was a dream town, a theme town for all movement is inauthentic. In fact I am beginning to think that reality is no longer relevant to our lives.

A conversation about two very famous people

Two ordinary people sit down and, over a cup of coffee, talk. They are just two people, a tabula rasa, you can make of them as you please for the only thing that you know is what you see and hear. They are both white, they are both men, not old, but not young either; trendy well-dressed men – this is what you see; and what you hear - the conversation that is recorded below.

Are they excited to speak of a town that is filled with energy; the energy of the newness of the old? Or do they live not in the now but in the past, not the past of the ordinary person, but the past of the famous and the exalted?

I went to Springs the other day, interesting place; old in that many of the building are Art Deco, and new, in that most of the residents there are recent immigrants. Went into the buildings and spoke to some of the people, the place is fascinating, to me that is, to others, I suppose, a cesspool.¬

The only exciting thing about Springs is that some very famous arty people came from the place.

What?

James Phillips and Nadine Gordimer; they both came from Springs.

Mmm, oh, didn't know that. I didn't go there looking for the famous anyhow, I just spoke to ordinary people.

So you were just looking at ordinary people, animals in the zoo even though your focus was on the cages, the Art Deco cages. Did they want your voyeurism?

Famous people, I figure that they like the voyeurism even if they don't say it, they like people to want them, to applaud them; that's my view anyway. I don't think that ordinary people want this; they just want to get on with their lives. I am an ordinary person and that's what I want.

Mmm you might have a point there, but then maybe not. I do want people to applaud me, so do you? Anyway tell more about these famous people. Nadine Gordimer, born in Springs, isn't she dead now?

Yes, 2014.

It's difficult to imagine her young, but the pictures that I have seen; she was gorgeous in her youth. There is that great picture of her in *The Guardian*, the article;

you can find it online; there she is holding a cigarette, sexy.

But by the time of the picture I think she had left Springs, she didn't stay there too long, lived with her parents until the big city of Johannesburg started fascinating her, there she stayed with her sister who lived somewhere in the Joburg suburbs. Springs was a time of her youth. Anyway the reason why I thought about you and your Springs interest was here, look, this magazine has a Springs feature; an article about Nadine Gordimer and one on James Phillips, or his alter ego *Bernoldus Niemand*.

What does that, *Bernoldus Niemand,* mean?

It means no-one. *Bernoldus* is a name, and then the surname, so it means *Bernoldus No-one*?

Read this, it's a fan letter. *I just wanted to charf you ous about this lekker CD that I scored the other day. It's called 'Wie is Bernoldus Niemand?' and is by a ou called Bernoldus Niemand. The tunes on this are like really cool and it says on the box that the ou lives in Springs because it gives him perspiration. It starts with a tune about him on the border and wanting to hug his Korporaal, now I'm not really into this whole homosapien thing, but jirre, sometimes out there you did just want to hug someone, so I can relate. The next song is like a weird one with old Bernoldus like telling about going into a bar in Springs looking for a jol, but it's like all in poetry and there's this like jazz type music playing, sings about his broken heart and sings to his cherry that he loves her for eternally. The ou at the shop also said that the ou singing on the CD was really that James Phillips ou who died, but I charfed him he was wrong because it says Bernoldus Niemand on the CD and James Phillips would nooit have done like those Milli Vanilla ou's.*

He had a lot of fans James did. But I can't relate, never found him that interesting.

Mmmm, yes, you don't like that kind of music, but also you don't like the unkempt, and he did look dirty.

I suppose he did think metaphorically. *Niemand,* the vacuity of white life, the violence and the need for the human

touch; are you saying that this makes him interesting?

No, I just liked his music.

You should say like, he might be dead but his music isn't.

How about another coffee?

What, yes please. They are both dead now. Nadine was ninety, I think she died in her sleep, peacefully as they always say, but I wonder how peaceful dying is. And James, he died young, a car accident, apparently he was fine afterwards but then he left the hospital and just died, must have had some kind of internal injuries.

They lived such contrasting lives didn't they?

I suppose both of them, in their different ways, experienced the violence of apartheid. But Nadine, I don't think experienced it directly; whereas James, he was in the army and there was a war, civil and outside the country, then. I don't think he fought at the border, but he had some experience of army life, maybe in the townships, and he always wrote about loneliness, the loneliness of the soldier who didn't know what he was fighting for.

It is interesting that you say that, in all Nadine's books, maybe I should say most of them not all, her white characters are bourgeois and beautiful, in fact she says it, look here; she acknowledges that she is a white colonial woman and that she knows her characters only through herself.

But she did know Mandela and spent a lot of time with Anti-Apartheid activists.

She was the white saviour?

Did you know she helped him, Mandela, to write and edit the speech that he gave from the dock at the treason trial, *I am prepared to die*?

No, I didn't; but it was more than moving, it was stirring. And his performance there, many young boys left the country because of that speech. And in movies that are made of him, it is always used, the great orator speaking from the dock. Didn't the one movie have Morgan Freeman in it?

I think so. She was a writer, a creator, she created through her imagination, and she created human beings with human failings, but at the same time she did acknowledge that in a society so polarised, as South Africa is, that people, writers included always fall back into playing roles, and so her characters act out preconceived roles, this is what is almost forced on them as it is the only frame of reference available.

I do think that you don't have to experience something to know it.

I suppose some will say that those who live in nice white houses with nice white gardens and nice white dogs were desensitised to apartheid violence. And yet I think that they are able to know it in their creativeness. If you are a person of ideas, if you know and mix with people who have ideas, then you can get to know them as equals, and then you can experience their pain and their good times, alongside your own.

Mmmm, possibly. Some say that James Phillips made his art and contributed to his death because he experienced this violence, and as a response he lived rough, drank, smoked, did drugs and made great music; the army, the psychosis of violence, which became drunken dagga-filled fucked late nights, no sleep, driving while drunk.

So what are you saying, those that have nice lives live for a long time?

No, those that have nice lives will always say wake up and take responsibility for what you do.

Nadine, she had a nice life, peaceful. I remember in an interview she said told the interviewer that in response to a young writer who said that he didn't read as books were so expensive that he should use the central library, she said this with words like 'my god, and for heaven's sake' so it was clear that she was horrified, a writer who did not read. It was easy for her to say take responsibility; very easy. So I think she only knew the violence of apartheid from her home in Parktown, and of course, her imagination.

So you are saying that James, irresponsible though he was, he knew this violence as he watched it all around him, was a part of it.

Maybe when he died he was tired of life? Could he imagine anything except the army and the defiance? Maybe that's what gave him meaning, and then when it was gone, he died just after the first democratic elections, there was nothing left for him to fight against.

Did you know that Nadine was the first South African who won the Nobel literature prize?

Naah. But tell me more about James.

He was born in Springs. He was a friend of a friend of mine's boyfriend. He used to describe, or she did, how he made the white trash of the East Rand his brand, his white working class trash brand. He loved Springs, or so I am told, the bars and the insalubrious white society who lived there.

Yes, listen to this; it's in this article, he describes a bar in the centre of Springs. It is next to a beautiful Art Deco building called Manitoba House, look here; here is a picture of it then, in the eighties with James standing smoking outside it. Didn't you go there the other day?

Yes, I did, but here in this picture it doesn't have the red painted balconies as it does now. Look, they are pink-ish, kind of pink and orange, peach.

Listen to this, it is a quote, apparently James said it, 'the building was the colour of a rotting peach, soft, because even as it was magnificent on the outside what was inside were the heads of rotten people, living in it and walking by, it stank'.

That picture was taken in the eighties; Springs, that building must have been filled with politics then, the politics of the violence that was inside people, men, boys, husbands.

And women.

Well it's the men that they picture here. I am sure they were all playing a role, a campy theatre role where they were brothers, brothers held together by their testosterone, their artifice, like the artfulness of the Art Deco buildings. Yes, I know the building, it is quite beautiful.

I like to compare the Art Deco buildings to music, but not James Phillips's music, his was more Afrikaner rock. No, Art Deco is romance, opulence, Mozart and Maria Callas.

That bar where he is standing in this picture, I don't think Maria Callas' voice was heard there. It's the real Springs, rough boys, mostly Afrikaans, and all of them, I imagine, talking about their experiences on the border or in the townships, the sounds of the wheels of the Casspirs going over people, that squishing hissing sound of blood and breath leaving a body, tears, a head snapping off a neck.

And of course, they must also have talked of women, that is where the women come in, their chicks, how they fucked them and were succoured by them.

I am thinking about real-ness. Real, what is the real Springs; my Springs, Nadine's, James's?

The real of then was that the only way those in the bar knew intimacy, knew touch, was through sex and violence, fucking and killing. That's the human contact they had, that's the only human contact they knew.

I could write a whole story on this, but it's been done before, so many times, the terrors and traumas of the young

white South African boys. It is annoying, it almost makes these boys or men into something we should feel pity for, and I don't really want to feel pity because they repel me. It is like feeling pity for a soldier in the German army in 1939. But back to James, maybe this is where his *Benoldus Niemand* songs came from, the bars, the Springs boys, the misery of the times. No, I'll write something else.

He was arrogant. Listen to what he says here, '*I am English, an English ou from Springs, but the album is in Afrikaans. I want to show that even Afrikaans people can sing of this horror, and anyway it is impossible to write about this stuff in English, my mother spoke English, it is like I don't want the language to be polluted, don't want to stain it.*'

He didn't want to stain his mother, how Freudian.

And real-ness for Nadine, she didn't speak about her experiences much even though she gave many interviews and wrote a great deal of non-fiction. I think she never really had them, as James did; hers were imagined and then translated into her novels. But look here, this article is all about her early years in Springs.

They did come from different times. Nadine lived in Springs in the 1940s and 50s, here she talks about what brought her parents to South Africa; her maternal grandfather came out from England to the diamond mines in Kimberley in the 1890s, South Africa then was the land of opportunity for Europeans, but from what she says he didn't make it as a diamond miner. Her mother was born here. And her father, her father was a poor Jew from Žagar, now Lithuania, he had hardly any schooling, here were the pogroms and his family was very big, he had to get out. So he came to South Africa. Her father knew the brutality of Russia, her mother, she did not know it in South Africa, no, I don't think that she knew the roughness of Springs, she was a colonial child. Nadine's experiences, and those of her sister, were those of a sheltered child. In Springs her father became quite well known, he at first was a watchmaker, all the Jewish immigrants were watchmakers, then he became the town's premier jeweller. I think she said that he would get on his bicycle and go from house to house asking if anyone wanted their watches fixed, then he employed his brother whom he brought from Russia to do this and stayed in his shop, it was in the centre of Springs, maybe you passed it. Did you know that

her father designed and made the mayor of Springs' mayoral chain?

No. They were Jewish, in Springs, surprising?

Yes. But you know then, while there may have been Anti-Semitism in the sense that the Jews were thought to be 'not like us', it was more the generalisation, 'all Jews are entrepreneurial or 'all Jews are artists'.

But there was Anti-Semitism, Afrikaans people would call out to the Jews on the streets 'you bleddy Jood', and they were thought of as 'not so much as entrepreneurial but mean money lenders, Shylocks.

I went to the synagogue; it's a beautiful building, surrounded now by barbed wire. I don't know if anyone uses it anymore. Someone said that it might have been an education centre now but there didn't seem to be anyone there when I went past.

I don't think that the Gordimer household was particularly religious. It seems from what I know and from what she wrote about in her essays, while the family did not reject Judaism, it was not something that made up their identity.

Didn't Nadine and her sister go to a convent in Springs?

Yes, maybe it was because there were no Jewish schools in the area and the convent was probably the best there was then.

I don't think she stayed there a long time, at some point she was kept home a lot, apparently her mother thought she had a weak heart. She didn't really get an opportunity to interact with the other children.

She was a dancer wasn't she? So after she was kept out of school she probably couldn't dance anymore.

She often speaks about how she resented her mother for stopping her dancing; the idea of movement, dance, is a motif in some of her books.

I wonder also if she was kept away from other children, other Springs children, as she was Jewish and her parents feared the Anti-Semitism among the Afrikaners.

No I don't think that they feared Anti-Semitism, as I said, the Jews were tolerated.

Although she did write about Anti-Semitism in a small town, didn't she?

She did, I remember *The Lying Days* and the way she described the Jews in it. I think this book, her first, was about Springs, or a small mining town like it.

Maybe that is why she became a

writer; the stereotype, the isolated child who was stopped from going to school, the child who needs a world to live in and so makes one up.

She did have her sister remember, but we don't hear too much about her, she was eclipsed by Nadine when she was young as Nadine was the one with the weak heart who needed constant care, and later in life as Nadine became the well-known writer.

The world of James Phillips, his Springs, it was very different to the Springs of Nadine. He doesn't appear to have had a sheltered life. He grew up working class, he always talks about his working class roots in interviews, but actually, I think, it was more the trade class. There were few white working class people, mostly people had trades; Afrikaans miners, immigrants who had set up the shops, barbers, bakers, clothing shops, that kind of thing.

So they, Nadine and James, they didn't live in those beautiful Art Deco buildings?

No, but many other immigrants did. They lived above their shops.

As they do now.

At that time, the eighties, when James was making it big, Springs was the hotbed of punk rock, the so called working class white boys who were either supportive of or damaged by apartheid, or the ones who resisted it and were therefore also damaged, they were the hip rockers then.

My view, for what it's worth; it was a good performance, the performativity of Springs, a small town boy who knew mortality and who now, as luck will have it, knows immortality.

Are we always all performing?

The theatre of life, ha, what a cliché!

Listen to this; *I'm a white boy who looked at his life gathered in his hands and saw it was all down to the life of some other man, the one who was shot down in the street. It is from one of James's songs, Shot Down.*

Done before!

Not then it wasn't. Apparently it was written after he had seen a photograph in the newspaper of a black man who had been shot in the street in Springs, a hard dry Highveld grass, the blood on the road.

Doesn't it remind you of *Blowing in the Wind,* maybe James was trying to be the Bob Dylan of Joburg? And look here, he says that *'I became aware that as a white person I had all the privileges, even though my folks were working class, I had education and a house and music lessons, things, and I had all this at the expense of*

the black people who were just shot down in the streets, just another body, could be an animal, a broken machine'.

Nice boy!

But not Jewish, wasn't Bob Dylan Jewish?

Mmmm. And then the song was used in a movie made by Andrew Worsdale, it was also called *Shot Down*, made in 1986.

I think James may even have been in the movie.

James, the boy from Springs who was fortunate enough to live in apartheid times and so he went to university, Wits University. That's called privilege.

This must have been the first time that he really mixed with black people. Not like the time when Nadine was at Wits, she was there for a year, back then black people were not allowed to study there without special permission so there were very few black students.

Yes she wrote about this in *The Lying Days*, a young black woman who was at the university and how she was one of the few black people there.

Aren't first books always autobio-graphical?

Does it matter?

I suppose it doesn't really matter whether it is autobiographical. Anyway Nadine didn't need the university to meet black people because after she dropped out she began to meet people who were involved in the Anti-Apartheid struggle, in Sophiatown, the photographers and the jazz musicians.

She was part of those white South Africans who empathised with black people but who never did give up any of their privileges. The only thing they may have done was to invite them, black people that is, illegally to their nice homes so they could sit in the garden under the trees.

Well, I won't give up my privileges. And neither will you.

The horror of the past has become a cliché. I am not saying that the past is, was, not sickening, but that this history has been recorded so often, in James's songs, in Nadine's books? I'm bored of it all.

And yet we must speak of it.

Perhaps the only way of finding any justice, if that is at all possible, is by telling stories over and over again, so that they come back, always, these stories, to haunt and shame us.

It's the stories that stay, not us, we die.

Nadine's first book was *The Lying Days*, as we were saying, it's about Springs

isn't it? It's all about small town life, the passion-less-ness of it, in her view there was no mental food, she was amazed how people could live like this, in a world with no ideas. She describes the trivialities in the conversations; women and household issues, men, golf or business. She wanted to feel life, not just live it, and no-one was there to share her ideas with so she wrote about them.

There is that line from Yeats that the title of the book is based on, the lines are in the beginning of the book; *Though the leaves are many, the root is one/Through all the lying days of my youth/I swayed my leaves and flowers in the sun/Now I may wither into the truth.*

If you know that Springs is where she grew up then you know that the book is based on the small town life of Springs; youth, the lying innocence, but also the lying idealism of the young, growing up in the sun, dancing in the sun, and then realising that this is all a lie. Many people have said that this book is autobiographical; Springs, the mines, the native shops at the edges of town run by Jews, moving to Joburg, young white people becoming involved in a struggle for justice.

I like the book; I think that it is the awareness that is valuable and important, an awareness of the separation between black and white, and also the awareness of prejudice, against black people, against Jews, against women. The woman, the main protagonist, Helen is her name, is privileged and sheltered, she is not Jewish she just knows someone who is, Joel, typical Jewish name, and so experienced this prejudice vicariously. And Joel's parents were such a stereotype, the stereotype of the immigrant Jewish family. Joel's parents had a native shop that was at the edge of town and his mother barely spoke as she didn't understand or speak much English and his father did not teach her. She cooked and kept house and of course, like all Jewish mothers, she loved her son.

Listen to this, I may not like all of her work but I do admire her construction, the way she constructed her words, her sentences, listen, it's so beautiful while at the same time being about such dull and banal things: *Statutes and laws and pronouncements may pass over the heads of the people whom they concern, but shame does not need the medium of literacy. Humiliation goes dumbly home – a dog, a child too small to speak can*

sense it – and it sank right down through all the arid layers of African life in the city and entered the blood even of those who could not understand why they felt and acted as they did, or even knew that they felt or acted.

If you think about it she could be writing about James; that bar in Springs, the rough types there who were unable to, or didn't want to understand their culpability.

It is as if all her characters were ashamed, they knew and felt ashamed, they carried this shame as one carries a bag, or a baby, on one's back. Their shame was their baggage, their hunch, hump. And that's it, James and the boys in the bar carried this shame too.

They are hunchbacks, and all the time they cover it up with bravado.

Why do you keep on saying they; why not us?

Bravado, the bravado of me and you and James and Nadine, and our inability to deal with this shame.

Tell me more about the book, *The Lying Days*.

It is about young white people in Johannesburg, and Helen's quietly developing disillusionment with them, and their inability to change anything, whether this was the politics of the country or their own domestic politics. But also it is about love. There is a great exploration of the love between Helen and Paul, Paul, in the book, was the man with whom Helen had a relationship. It is a beautiful exacting description of this love; the first heady days, then the succumbing to the daily tedium of domesticity, and then the rising tensions of being too close. The main theme of the book is estrangement, and how imagination fails us.

Aren't we always estranged from others?

Apartheid was, and this book says it in so many words, in so many ways, an immense failure of the imagination; the failure to imagine ourselves into the skins and lives of others, the failure to imagine touching another. Her descriptions are vivid, the awfulness real, the awful realness.

Can we translate imagination into reality, as Nadine did?

We don't have to, we have fiction as our reality, her fiction, it makes us remember, it keeps us remembering, we remember what we do not know.

I live with my shame.

Maybe James died of shame.

And Nadine; or was she too old to be ashamed?

Can we ever know each other?

Can we know the people in the conversation, Nadine Gordimer, James Phillips, you and me?

Can we remember?

And remember me. I am famous too!

Penelope Heyns, me, remember me, I am a South African gold medal winner, sport, yes sport, you don't know sport do you? I never wrote a book or a song. Is that why you don't remember me?

But I am a famous person. And I was born in Springs.

Did you know that in 1992, at the Barcelona Olympic Games, I was the youngest member of the South African swimming squad? And then in 1994 I represented South Africa in the Commonwealth Games where I won a bronze medal in the two hundred metres. And then I represented South Africa in the Olympic Games in Atlanta. Here I won both the one hundred metres and the two hundred breaststroke events. This made me the only woman in the history of the Olympic Games to do so.

I bet you didn't know any of that? And I bet that you didn't know that I was South Africa's first post-apartheid Olympic gold medallist.

I think, no I know, that I am the world's greatest woman breaststroker of all time.

I'm too old now to swim for my country; yes I call it my country. I am patriotic.

Springs is not the same place that I was born in, but I still love my country and if I could I would still swim for it.

Now I teach swimming to young children. They can swim for the country in the Olympic Games. And I am a motivational speaker. I think all children, the blacks and the whites, can be inspired by what I did then, and what I do now. I like to give people confidence, confidence in themselves and their country.

Will we ever know Penny Heyns?

Can we remember?

To: B
From: A
Re: Springs
...

Hello again. It has been quite a while since we last communicated with each other; or maybe when I last communicated with you for you do not communicate. I write to a fictional you, someone who is not there, but you are in the words, on the pages, and I know that you are there, here, somewhere in the ether. You are like those strange emails we, or should I say I, sometimes receive, the ones where I have no idea who the sender is but they have managed to get my mail address and are sending me mysterious stuff, like pornography or religious tracts or self-help courses, stuff that I might want to buy. And so you are out there, enigmatic, covert, waiting. I think that I like to write to you for I have no-one else to write to, and that I do want to write because writing is movement. The movement of fingers as they touch the computer keys, a b or an A or an mb, or the movement of my hand as it strokes the page if I write with a pen, droplets of ink on a white page, a eulogy on a shroud, the death of this Art Deco town. Anyway movement, I think about the movement of the people as they walk outside my flat, as I sit and watch a woman who is dressed in a bright Igbo design, or a young man in a white kurta who wears a red fez, or a child in a T shirt, African, not African? They walk in the dirt of the town, silhouetted against the beautiful, what is a better word for beauty, lovely, magnificent, buildings, should I not use a word at all and merely describe the buildings or it is the buildings that I think are beautiful? People, they are too animate to be beautiful. And as I think about the movement below me and watch it and an awful lot of stuff comes to my mind, lots of disparate stuff. I think often about ballet, I am reading up on the different choreographers and the formal forms of ballet creations. Did you know that the Art Deco designs and ballet often went together, Diaghilev created set designs for Stravinsky's Rite of Spring, the one in which Nijinsky dances, the performance that was howled and booed off the Paris stage, but supported and loved by Coco Chanel, she was so excited by it that it inspired her to have a love affair with Stravinsky, was developed in a decorative and extravagant way, the Art Deco of the moment. And Nijinsky in this performance executed the complex ballotté, this is a jumping step that consists of a series of jumps performed with a rocking and swinging movement with the leg extended at either 45 or 90 degrees. It is a very difficult step, and Nijinsky had to practise if over and over again, for weeks, Diaghilev drove him almost out of his mind, well he did didn't he? It is the loss of 45 degrees, of the loss of 90 degrees, the movements of loss, the 45 degree or 90 degree loss of the decorations in this town that occupies me. I wonder why I want these buildings, this brick and mortar which is only eighty or so years old, to survive? It makes me unhappy that they will probably not survive, yes the buildings will be there but the decorative forms will disintegrate, destroyed by neglect and economics. And then I think about the rain forests, they are more than millions of years old, and I don't worry much about their destruction. But moving onto another subject, I also think about Andy Warhol. I think about him because while I do not wear a wig, I have a silver hair that falls in much the same way as his does across my forehead, but also because I bought a book on Edie Sedgwick who is a slippery sliver of beauty. And then I read that Andy Warhol, who was the precursor or maybe prediction- ist, is there such a word, of our consumer driven society, loved Art Deco furnishings. I am sure that he loved the buildings too, after all he did live in New York. He

• • •

was an active and known collector of Art Deco. He shopped for decorative artefacts at thrift stores and once made a special trip to Europe to find a particularly fabulous and famous Ruhlmann, this is a sinuously contoured chiffonier made of amboyna wood. In the pictures of his flat, I suppose he would have said apartment, there is also a Pierre Legrain pair of console tables, they are easy to identify as their tops and block feet are veneered with galuchat, or sharks' skin. And he was aware that all this decoration was ephemeral, art is an adventure of the mind. And so the conundrum, as I walk the streets of Springs and look at the buildings and watch the people I know that it is an art adventure for me, every day is art. So that's it, I want the buildings to survive while I am alive so that I can have the art adventure by just being in the streets, I am here, I am not in the rain forest, there is no adventure there, for others, but not for me. People often ask me why I continue to live here, they are always saying oh Springs, it is falling apart and that's when I turn to Warhol and ask what would you say? And he says I never fall apart because I never fall together. And I say that's me. Nothing falls apart, not these buildings nor me, and yet nothing falls together either, not these buildings or me. I dwell often on the consumerist theme, maybe because someone suggested making Springs into a theme park where tourists can come and look at the buildings, or maybe it was when another suggested holding a fashion show here. Both of these ideas I think are great, as long as the people can stay and will not be adversely affected. Does this sound far too liberal and caring to you? Anyway Warhol reflected the two great themes of his time, my time, your time, the mass consumption of goods and the industrialisation of people, particularly celebrities, and isn't this what a fashion show and a theme park do, everything becomes something to consume and the celebrities involved can be bought and sold? Money, let's make it, I need to make it, and good business is the best art, Andy knew this. He is Mary Magdalene; the holy whore of art who sold himself and accepted the attention of the exploitative public which buys the artist rather than the art, and the artist is always perfectly willing to admit that his art is trash. All the buildings here are trash, they are being trashed, literally, and I, I venerate them for I believe that they are art, not homes, but art, and so what, people buy the art, or rent it, to make a home. So maybe I will just respond to the events of our times and know that the Art Deco buildings which are now broken never really had any content, they were just homes, the content was shelter, and on the shelter there is style, depoliticised and disengaged, home. And now they are another home, as they have always been, to the zany lives of the children, the children of Springs.

A Story of Children

Leah: I want to be a singer, I want to be Beyoncé and go to places in America. You can buy a lot of things in America, like iPhones. Watch me dance.

Daren: I am from Zimbabwe, not here, my mother told me, but I can't remember what that place where I was born is like. My mother says that is a good place, there is just no work for my father and for her to do so we can't get money there. That's why we came here. I don't need to work, I go to school, I am ten. I like this building. I like the round windows, windows aren't round you know, they are square, only these ones are round, and I like that they are red. Look there, look, at Tatendo, he is my friend, look at how he is looking from that window, he looks like a bird that pokes its head from a hole in a tree, a tree where the bird lives, we live in this place like it is a tree, the hole is round like these windows, and look, look at him looking at us. Tatendo, he can fly, he told me this, so at night he flies from the window, he is like a space ship, or maybe a bird. I wish I could fly. I can remember the birds from Zimbabwe, there were a lot of them there. They were not black like Tatendo, he is a Zulu, they were green and red and some were even purple, and some were all of those colours. My mother has some of the feathers; she says it reminds her of the mountains there, she keeps them in a box at the back of the cupboard or sometimes she puts them on a hat when she goes to church. My mother says that when we go inside our room we must always lock the door because sometimes there are bad people in this place, they will steal, and sometimes they kill people from Zimbabwe, but I have never found them, all the people here are my friends. Look there, that lady, she helps my mother with the washing, she is Tatendo's sister, she can't fly like he can, but she is nice. My father has a good job here, no I don't know what he does, something with cars, he earns money so I can go to school, and then he can also send some of this money to his mother who lives in Bulawayo.

Tatendo: Cool butti.

Abigail: I have just completed Grade 12 at the Springs Girls High School, now I want to be a model, or a dancer. Do you know any agencies that I can send my CV to? My reading is good; I read fashion magazines and also, what, yes I read African books, ones that are written by Africans. Look, *Things Fall Apart*, it's broken now, some pages are not here, my teacher gave it to me, I have read it, and look, look at how I can walk, like a real model walks, look at me. The Congolese salon down the road, yes down there, they did my braids, but it was expensive.

Tshepo: My father drinks, and even his girlfriend does too. Sometimes so do I, I drink when he is not looking, because even though he does not really notice me he still says I must not drink because then I will drink all of his drink. So I take his drink. It does not really taste nice but I like to drink because then my whole room becomes very bright and always, every time, an angel comes to sit on top of my bed. He is white and has very wide wings, but sometimes when he sits on the shelf in the corner there he folds them up so you can't notice them. He sits there, where the chilli sauce is, he is white, like you. Do you have wings? He can fly, sometimes he flies around the room, he can fly in the dark or in the light, he is not big, but sometimes when he flies past me I can feel his wings on my face, they are not soft like you think, they are hard, like a chicken bone. He can't break these wings because then he won't be able to fly anymore and then he will be stuck in my room, like he is in jail. And I don't think he wants to go to jail, my father has been to jail and he says it is not nice, people fight and you don't get nice food there. Sometimes I ask him, the angel, he is called Mark, if he also wants to taste the drink but he always says no, he says no because then maybe he will damage his wings and then he won't be able to fly and also because if he drinks he can't see straight. My father says this sometimes, he says 'I can't see straight' and then he just falls asleep. I like Mark the angel; he talks to me and then I don't feel lonely anymore.

Ntabileng: I am here today because my sister is sick and I need to take care of her. But on most days I am in Kwa-thema, I go to the college there where I am studying to be a boiler maker. It is a two year course and then I get the certificate, and then I can go and get a job with a big business that does building. Sometimes I practise here, here in this building because sometimes the water is not hot and I need to fix the boiler, it is below the ground, just underneath, I have to get there through that door there, but now it is locked. The boiler

down there is not new, it is rusty. I think this building needs to get a new one.

Perfection, of a kind, was what he was
after,
And the poetry he invented was easy to
understand;
He knew human folly like the back of his
hand,
And was greatly interested in armies
and fleets;
When he laughed, respectable senators
burst with laughter,
And when he cried the little children
died in the streets.

Karl: I want to be a builder when I get bigger and build buildings like this one. The guy that is the owner of this building, he comes from another country, I don't know which one, but he says in the place where his family is from, his mother and his father, they still live there, there are a lot of buildings like this one, they are decorated with round windows and colours, there is even one that looks like an aeroplane he says, it used to be owned by a garage, or a car maker, I am not sure. He says that if I am a builder I can fix up all these buildings here and they will become better, better to live in, but also better to look at, so that then I can charge you money to come and look at them. You can't then just come in for free. I can make a lot of money if I was
a builder.

Pretty: This place is my house, it is small, my auntie tells me that when she was growing up she lived in a place where there were trees and cows, and a lot of space in the house, but I, I don't know this kind of thing, I just live here. It feels nice to me because when I sit inside my room, we have one room me and my auntie, then I feel safe, no-one can come and get me or kill me, or make me do things that I don't want to do. I like it when there is no-one in the room, just me because then I can think of what I will look like when I am big and soon I will be big and I will be very beautiful. The room helps me not to be sad because it hugs me and I can put pictures on the walls.

Xavier: When we came here, I came here with my brother, I was glad because then when we walk to the Kentucky Chicken place we do not worry about anyone shooting us or that there will be a bomb in the Kentucky. Once in the place where I came from a bomb went off in the shop where I was, the owner and two of the people inside there were killed, their heads blown off, I was lucky I only got cut on my arms and

shoulder, look here, the scar, and look, I can't lift my arm so well but it's OK I'm not going to climb any trees, there are no trees here except the ones carved into the bricks at the entrance.

Xoliswa: Sometimes when I am here, standing just here, yes just here at the top of the stairs, I can see a shadow that slides down that wooden rail side next to the stairs, the rail on the wall, it is a spirit of one of the children that used to live here, one of the children who is dead now. The shadow, it never comes close to me, but when I wave at him, it is a boy, I know this, he waves back to me. I think he is lost because even though he used to live here he is dead now, and other people live here so he does not know it this is the right place to come back to. But when I wave at him I also smile, look, I have only one front tooth, the other fell out, I knocked it out, and then he knows that I am his friend and he can come here whenever he wants to. I wish that he would talk to me because then I would learn about when he was small and his life from long ago.

Daniel: I come from Nigeria. I remember the big river there right in the place where I was born.

Essop: And I come from Pakistan, that's where Osama Bin Laden is from. That's where the Americans killed him. My dad says I must pray every day, so I do, and when I pray I always face that way, yes that way, up there. Sometimes when I am praying I forget to think of God and think of Pretty, she is my girlfriend.

James: I think we must love everyone
Norman: We must hate the criminals.

On my school notebooks
On my desk and on the trees
On the sands of the pavement
I write your name
On the fields, on the horizon
On the birds' wings
And on the shadows
I write your name
On the froth of the cloud
On the sweat of the storm
On the dense rain and the flat
I write your name
On the flickering figures
On the bells of colours
On the natural truth
I write your name
On my dog, great hearted and greedy
On his ears
On his paws
I write your name
For I was born to know you

To name you
Liberty

Rethabile: I do all the washing in this building, and I do it every day, well not all of the days but most of them. And sometimes I get money for it, and then I give the money to my mother. She says that this all helps to feed the household, her and my two brothers and sometimes my father. I hang the washing there, on that line, I like the different colours, sometimes I hang it in different patterns so that I make a picture of the different colours. Take a photograph then you can send it to me, or send it to that guy there, on his phone. Maybe you can put the picture in the Mall, they have a lot of pictures there of these places, there is one of this building. Wait, wait, let me stand right next to this line, you can see the colours
then properly.

Winifred: In Lesotho we have a lot of water and sometimes it gets very cold, not like here, here, even on a cold day like today it is hot. Sometimes it snows there. Sometimes I dream of going back there and riding on a pony, let me show you this picture, this one, this pony.

Jimmy: Sometimes I dream of being a soldier with a gun, I can shoot people then. When I go inside my room I can dream there and no-one interrupts me, it's peaceful, I can shoot people and no-one disturbs me, not even the TV.

Scott: Where I was before I came here there were many people with guns, sometimes I heard them when I was sleeping, my mother died by a gun, and my sister, then my father fought the men with guns and killed them all. There was a lot of blood; it looked like many cows were slaughtered in the yard that day.

Ann: I like animals. I am a vegetarian. My mother says I should eat meat but I don't want to because there is this mouse that is my pet. This mouse, I call him Obama after the American President, he came from Kenya, my country. Anyway my mother says Obama is a rat, no not the President, but I think he is a mouse because he is friendly and rats are not friendly, they eat people's noses when they are sleeping and even sometimes they eat their whole eyes out of their heads and then they are blind. But this mouse, Obama, sometimes I call him Michael, or it might be another mouse that is in the room, after Michael Jackson, he has a fluffy tail, and he sometimes runs up my arm and hides in this hole here, this one, the one at my shoulder, look, he is here now, he is peeping out. I feed him pieces of bread and sometime porridge. He sleeps in a hole in the wall; it goes all the way through the wall to the outside. When he goes inside there I wonder if he will come back, and he always does. Not like my brother, he is older than me, he went away and he never came back. I think that he is dead, that's what my mother says.

I keep all the old photographs from then,

someone will want them one day, it's history you know, my history.

Let me tell you about this one, look. I will tell you the story of this picture, or some of the story because I can only remember some of it, and I can't really describe things so well, feelings, I can't remember my feelings then.

It was in Pioneer Park, yes I remember, the picture was taken in Pioneer Park.

It is an old picture; and it is faded.

The picture is in black and white, a sad picture, not because it is faded, or because it shows the wicked-ness of the world, it is a wicked world and the park is filled with roses, but because it is a picture of dead people, except for the woman who told me the story. Dead people who must have picked the roses in the park, and said the words *Roses are Red, Violets are Blue, Sugar is Sweet and so are You,* and they believed that they were good people, and they believed in the beauty of the roses and they believed that the world was not wicked and that they could never die.

The picture; there are five people in it, three of them are men, Morné, John and Derick, and two are woman, Christa and Jill. And they are all dressed as if someone asked them to dress somewhat formally, in a way that will show whoever is looking at the picture that they are serious young people. They are not dressed as if they are in a park and it is hot, they are almost unreal, surreal, for they do not smile, nothing gives them away, nothing tells us that they will die.

Christa is wearing a pant suit, she is dressed entirely in white but for her shirt and scarf. The jacket and the trousers are white, underneath this whiteness is a black and white striped shirt, and around her neck is a black and white scarf. At her neck a small amount of skin shows through, where the shirt buttons can close, but they are not, is a scarf, it is tied into a V shape. The scarf has a tail; it is on the left of the white skin of her neck. The neck is elongated, strangle-able, but the scarf does not strangle it decorates.

Christa has long blonde hair, but because the picture is black and white it is difficult to know what colour her eyes are, they may be blue, they probably are blue for her hair is blonde and her skin is light. Her hands are clasped, one over the other, and her legs are crossed one over the other, both on the

same side; the right side. She holds something in her left hand; the devil's hand, something close to the photographer, a rose, it may be a red rose that she picked in the park for there are a lot of roses in the park landscape that is behind and in front of her, roses from a queen's garden. Her eyes are closed, or half closed. She shows nothing except her vacancy. An imaginary conversation with her might go something like this:

> Christa: Hi Morné.
> Morné: Oh, hi.
> Christa: Morné.
> Morné: Hmmmm
> Christa: I ...
> Morné: What?
> Christa: I thought ....
> Morné: What were you saying?
> Christa: Nothing.

Around her left wrist is a bracelet, it could be gold, and on her left hand, the third finger of the left hand, is a silver ring.

Morné faces slightly to the left, he is close to Christa, but not that close; he does not look at her, you do not know where he looks for he is wearing dark glasses. He may be looking at the rose that Christa holds, or the grass of the park, or the building that is somewhere to the left of all the people in the photograph. He is distant.

Is the sun shining Morné?

Morné wears dark glasses.

Morné is dressed for the cold Highveld winter. His dark jacket is leather. Underneath this he wears a grey shirt. His neck is visible as he does not wear a scarf. He wears black pointed boots; they look like Chelsea boots, boots made in America. The only lightness that is visible is his skin, and his hair, his grey blonde hair that falls over his left eye, the eye that is hidden behind the glasses.

Morné stares at the camera; he is the centrepiece, the most important person in the picture.

John is also in grey and black. He too stares into the distance; he looks over Morne, in front of him, at something that is not Morné. His arms are folded; he holds truth close to his body and his boots, his possibly Chelsea boots, come up high. His trousers are tucked into his boots, as if they need to be secure. His shirt, a T shirt, has a round neck and is

striped horizontally. John is reed thin. John also wears dark glasses. And he also holds a rose, a red rose.

All the men wear dark glasses.

Only the women do not wear dark glasses.

Jill stands behind Morné, nothing but her elfin face is perceptible, and her left leg. Her body is effaced by Morné, his dark clothes and his white body engulf her slimness.

Derick grips the back of a chair, his fingers wrap around the metal tightly, it is easy to know this for his knuckles are lighter than the skin of his fingers, than the skin of his arms, they are white tipped. He wears light coloured trousers, they are slightly darker than the colour of his white skin which is beige. On his jaw is a shadow, as if he has not shaved for a few days, or is it the shadow of the rose that John holds out? *Roses are Red Violets are Blue, Sugar is Sweet and so are You.*

Morné, John and Derick all wear dark clothing. And so does Jill. Only Christa is dressed in white.

They stand just outside a building in Pioneer Park in Springs. Behind the building is a wall with a gate in it, the gate is closed.

There is a sign on the gate, white lettering on a black background. It says 'Swimming Pool/Swembad/Careful/Versigtig'.

This is Pioneer Park, a place for weddings and birthdays and anniversaries and baptisms. Morné and Jill and John and Derick and Christa are celebrating but they do not smile. It could it be a birthday celebration but they fear growing old, and their death which is coming closer as they age, or it could be because soon a change will come to Springs and the roses will die.

The floor of the building where they stand is made up of rectangular white tiles; behind them is a glass plated door, in it the park is reflected, some trees and the many rose bushes, there are roses on these bushes so it is probably not winter for the plants are blooming. But the roses are not important; they are just there, growing in the park, only the faces of the people in the photograph are memorable, they play in the mind for this photograph will never be taken again.

Who are Morné and John and Jill and Derick?

I can't remember.

But I remember the park.

So the word person
means a
human being?
Yes?
It means this in most
European languages;
and the word persona
means an
actor's mask.

No-one reveals himself as he is; we all wear a mask and play a role.

Christa and Jill and Morné
and John and Derick are
actors in the playtime
of Springs.
And the park, it is filled with roses.

To: B
From: A
Re: Springs

...

Hi there, stranger, I have not heard from you for a while, it seems like years, but it is probably only months, or even weeks, time goes very slowly when you are enjoying yourself and I like to think that I am enjoying myself in this strange small town. It is strange how I think about words. Why, I wonder, is it strange for I am a writer? Anyway the word strange has been in my thoughts, strange, bizarre, foreign, I look it up in a dictionary, try to find a meaning; I try to find synonyms in the thesaurus. Strange, the stranger, the word has been in the news a lot, there is a lot of violent violence, the deliberate rather than random killings of foreign people, the shooting and eating of foreign birds, the removal of foreign plants and trees, invasive aliens and weeds, an attempt to rid this place of anything that is perceived as menacing. And so I think about this strange place that I live in, this strange place called Springs for it is filled with strange aliens. We have alien people, many, the percentage is at least twenty, of the people who live in the town are alien, and this figure will double in the next twenty years if no action is taken to eradicate them, or here are they referring to the plants I can't be certain? Yes, there are also alien plants, and alien birds, and alien buildings. I am sitting on the balcony of one of these buildings now, Manitoba House, and looking into another, the old Palladium theatre, I can just make out the crenulations on the roof, and four, no six of the curling letters that make up the word Palladium, and then underneath, and next to what were words is a date, it is carved three times into the wall, underneath the name, and to the right and left of it, but all the dates are different now, 1..5.. and 195.. and 1955, for some of the numbers have fallen down. Some of this alien building has been eradicated, but this is indecorous and a slap to the civilised. I look at aliens every day, when I walk down the street to the chemist, the man who is the security guard at the chemist, Charles, is an alien, he is from Senegal, or when I just sit on the balcony and look down, Ishmael, as in the same name Ishmael from the novel *Moby Dick*, works downstairs, he does not touch me, he will not shake my hand, for a Muslim man does not touch a woman, but once when I fell, I stumbled over some broken paving, he helped me to get up and I learnt then that a Muslim man can touch a woman if she looks to be in need of help, he comes from Pakistan, and his wife, when I see her, wears black and only her blue eyes are visible. Aliens, that word again, when I look closely at the pavement, in between the cracks there are weeds, alien weeds, or when I open my ears and listen to the birds, the Myna bird, an African Grey Parrot that has escaped from somewhere, everything, everywhere, there is an alien. And who and where and what are these aliens? I think that new things, people or birds or plants are alien, because new is threatening and so they are called invasive. Also aliens have a nasty habit of hybridising with native species, a Nigerian marries a South African, the green-headed yellow-billed mallard duck in Pioneer Park breeds with the white faced whistling ducks that swim there, pure ducks are being replaced by mallard-white-faced duck hybrids, the pure South African is being replaced by a Sigerian or maybe a North Nafrican. Depending upon when and who things are written about so the narrative changes, it can be welcoming, as the strange and foreign buildings are welcomed, or feral and menacing, as the Nigerians and the mallard ducks are menacing, as is the purple flowering jacaranda that grows outside the fire station and is sucking the soil dry and the roses in Pioneer Park that are now dead

● ● ●

and which have been replaced by Lantana and bug weed, beautiful and intricate if you look at it closely, but alien, a serious threatening invader. Did you know that invasive plants, yes the word invasive is used, suck water from the ground when there is little to distribute, we live in a dry Highveld climate, and invasive people remove billions of cubic metres of water from our water reserves each year. A politician the other day said that we will pay a hideous price for this invasion, for this ignorance. Was he referring to plants or people or birds? Birds, I have heard are major pests that compete with and threaten the country's indigenous species, is this the same for people? Foreigners compete with and seriously threaten the countries indigenous people? The negative impacts of these aliens include damage to property, who damages the Art Deco buildings, the birds or the people? Feral pigeons roost in the curlicues and spread harmful bacteria by shitting everywhere. Somalia people, people from Bangladesh, Sudanese people, they shit too, maybe they too spread harmful bacteria? I read somewhere that some aliens did not survive, the colonists tried to introduce game birds like pheasants, did you know that a chicken, the common chicken whose thighs and breast you eat is part of the pheasant family, he comes from India, he is an alien, he is eaten, for hunting, and song birds like nightingales that reminded them of England, but these introductions were unsuccessful, the colonists were forced to move on, Onward Christian Soldiers, now there are other aliens, they evict the birds from their nests. Aliens, alienation, this is ballet movement; the déboulés, a fast sequence of half turns performed by stepping onto one leg, and completing the turn by stepping onto the other, it is performed on the balls of the feet or high on the toes, with the legs held very close together, was introduced into the Russian ballet by Cossacks. Diaghilev introduced it onto the Paris stage, and now it is part of the oeuvre. It is a complex movement that requires resilience and stamina, but when executed, is exceptionally beautiful. Are aliens that bad? How can they be executed?

I dream about home.
Why?
Because my home,
the sweat, the blue
ocean, the palm trees,
the crows, my home, it
shelters my dreams.
Your dreams, what dreams?
At home I can dream;
I can dream in peace,
I can daydream, my
home protects
my dreams.

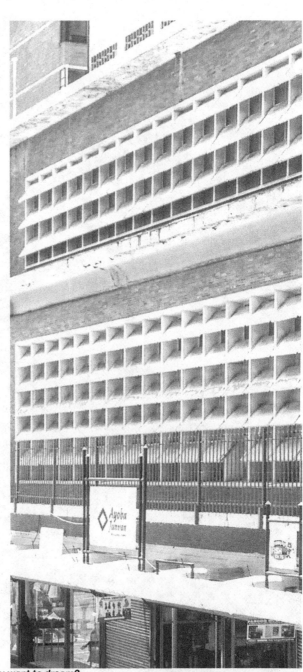

Why do you want to dream?
Because I want a home.

The Palladium theatre, the largest theatre

in the East Rand, was built in 1937. But it is no longer a theatre; it is a space, a space where people live. It is made up of rooms, dry walled, one bathroom, one kitchen. The screen where once movies were shown has been removed, some say torn down by people who are no more than animals, others say removed for it took up the space needed for living in. Now there are no movies shown on the screen, now they are three-dimensional performances, and the film is still in black and white but it is no longer silent.

WATCH

WAIT

LISTEN

Music: Piotr Llich Tchaivosky, the 1812 Overture.

Credits: White writing on a black background that is covered in sparkling red and yellow stars.

Performers and Director: All of Us

Inside the Palladium theatre:

In one of the rooms, it measures two meters by one meters, is a plastic desk and an upright plastic chair. A blanket is on the floor and a pillow stands upright next to the door. On the desk are pieces of paper, scattered and torn. The paper is covered in writing, marked, the mark of Cain furrows his dark forehead, the written word, symbols, lines drawn in black, a picture of something, not a flower or a bird, an abstract drawing, human. To the left of the desk, high up on the wall, is a window, opaque bars of black metal cut through the glass. He picks up a pen, writes, a beam from the outside glows blue in the twilight; a waxing moonlight traces the contours of the bars. The light in the room is not turned on, the unlit globe casts a moon shadow on the wall in front of him, as he turns he catches its reflection, it dances in the windowpane, mocking. He bends his head to look at the pages of words, a tawny insect walks across one of them; it drags its right back leg, wings folded down, a shroud on the white paper. He places his palm on the insect and squashes it flat, dirt on the page, another word, another picture.

Cut to outside.

Outside the window, about two meters from where he sits, a half-naked body lies on a concrete bench, it does not move as he looks at it. A figure crosses the road and moves towards the inert body. The moving figure stops, it is still, he looks, a pen hovers in the air, an invisible string guides it downwards towards the page. The bars of the window move in, they enclose the standing figure, then cover the face, a black line across the eyes. His hand that holds the pen lingers, the hand above the motionless body is raised, its fingers curl, rigid, a blade, written, the knife moves slowly, into a heart. He watches the body shudder upwards, a light movement, the light skin is caught in the wind, it breathes then it is breathless. The body lies on the concrete bench, liquid seeps, it wells upwards, then it drops, a finger pricked by a needle, a tear that flows from an eye. Blood spots drop onto the concrete floor, splatter.

Camera returns to him, close up:

In the half-light he can make out the picture that the spots cause, a little mermaid, her tail flips, then it flaps, then it is still. Legs grow from the tail and begin to walk towards him but he cannot see them now, it is too dark and the bars of the window bisect his vision; first there are three legs now there are two, and then there are two words on the white page.

Outside:

The sirens in 3rd Street: police cars, blue lights, tyre marks that scream, brakes clash and crash as if they are the waves in an ocean, running men in blue, hand guns, bullets blend into wooden walls, become decoration, a coat hook.

The child who is dressed in a pink dress that reaches to her knees so that it covers the end of her long white socks holds a woman's hand. The woman is tall. They stand together next to the window of the electronics shop that also sells bridal wear and watch this movie; they must wait for it to finish, for the action to outrun itself, before they can go up the stairs of the theatre and into the room where they live. Here, as she does every evening when she and the child return home, the woman will turn on the television and watch the News of the World as she cooks a meal of dead chicken and spinach.

THE END

Mother As-Salam-u-Alaikum

I know that you worry about me and that you think about me, yes, I am far away, but I am well and always if I think of home then the second thing that I think of is always you, it is only Allah, Glory to him, the Exalted, that I think of before I think of you. The thing is down here I can't be writing to you all the time, I have a lot to do, and also, while I may have the internet on my phone my sister Rafi does not so she has to go down the road to the internet café to download the mail that I send to you. Soon I will send money for the air tickets for you all.

Anyway you know that I have always been a wanderer, and so I wandered here, and this place is good, sometimes, it is horrible, dirty, dirtier than the Ravi Road where I lived with you, although some of Lahore is not clean, but you know, you taught me how important it is to keep our places clean and here there are so many people who are not Muslim that it is impossible to keep it clean. Also sometimes, not so much these days, but sometimes the people here gang up against foreigners and sometimes they are violent. It is not so much with us, the Asians, it is more often those who come from Africa; it is as if we are all not already in Africa and are Africans.

My shop does well. I have all the fancy goods that people like to buy, good quality. In fact yesterday I got a big consignment of goods from my friend who lives in Benoni, another town that is close by Springs where I live. He is Mustapha, Mr Cassim, the neighbour but one from where you are in Ravi Road's, nephew. His uncle, not Mr Cassim from Ravi Road, he is still in Lahore, but another one supplied both of us with some very good stuff. I work in my own shop, but next door in another shop is a guy from Lagos, he also sells stuff, and often we share what consignments we get. I sold him some of these new goods. Sometimes people say to me why is your shop next door to someone else who sells the same things as you do and I tell them if people are looking they will look at both and I can persuade them to buy from me.

And so I am fine and so is Merriam, and both the children are doing well. Merriam stays home with them; she must take care of that which is precious to all of us.

We live in this building called Renesta House. It is owned by a Muslim family; they are very rich and do not live here in Springs where we live. They have a clothing shop in the building on the ground floor and they rent out the flats above this. The building is on the main road, so sometimes it is very noisy, but never as noisy as the place where I grew up with you in the Ravi Road, but sometimes at night we have to keep our door locked and we do not go outside for it sounds as if there are things happening that are dangerous, shouting and sometimes gun shots. Some of the flats are big and others are small, we have a small one, it was once a big flat but it has now been divided up into two, so we have to share a bathroom with our neighbours but it is fine because they are also Muslim and are clean. We do not need more space than what we have here. There is even a small area in the corridor downstairs where we can look out from a window that is made of stained glass, it faces the holy city of Hejazi and so it is very good for prayer. Where I put my prayer mat the floors are made of real marble and there are coloured tiles on the walls; the owner has not taken them away. Merriam and the other Muslim women who live in the building keep this place clean. I try to do the Salat five times per day, sometimes this is difficult because I am busy, but I believe that Allah, the Grace of Allah be upon me, will forgive me. When I do not pray I think of the words that you always told me when I was a young child: 'Woe to those who pray, but are unmindful of their prayer, or who pray only to be seen by people' and am aware that I must not pray if I am not fully devoted or if I have other things on my mind at the time of prayer.

I do not have many friends here so often I just talk to Merriam and the children, and the man who works in the shop next door for he is Muslim.

I have nothing else to tell you now.

Tell father that I hope that he is well and that he must go down to the Western Union in two weeks' time as I will be able to send money to you then.

Your son Rashid

The blue lights swirl, round and around and around, the sirens scream, round and around and around, two white Toyota Corollas and three white vans that have the words South African Police written in blue

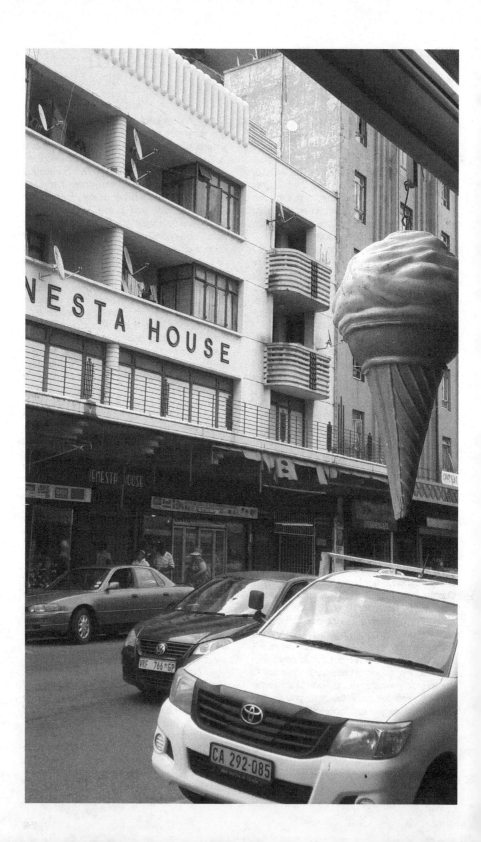

down both sides travel fast, very fast. The road, 3rd Avenue, is filled with cars; they swerve and groan as they slip over to one side to allow for the white cars to pass by. The police cars travel in one line, one white car follows another, the blue lines on their sides blur into one as if the sky is streaking past. After five blocks the cars come to a halt, tyre rubber sparks. Doors open, from each car steps a policeman, then a second, the back of each van opens and four policemen jump out. There are sixteen men on the pavement now.

Hey Nigerian uya kuphi?

U-Paki uthola u-fuck uphume lapho futhi afike lapho lowo mbhikisho uBin Laden ekhona khona.

Kuyini lo hey, yini fuck?

I-Fakes wena ubopha ama-bastards, i-Nike hey fake, i-Caterpillar eyinqaba, konke okukhohlisayo.

Hhayi wena awusiye ngisho ne-Afrika, uthole i-fuck out kuleli zwe wena waseNigeria.

A crowd gathers. Shadows decorate the vertical balusters and the geometric shapes become mysterious magical angels that move upwards and fly downwards as water in a fountain does, and the rounded balconies become square as the silhouettes of people dance in and outside the windows.

A thin Asian man who wears a turban on his head as Mohammed once did walks away from Renesta House.

A black man lies on the pavement. He bleeds from his forehead, his chest is caved in and a femur protrudes from his right leg. Then he sits up, his hand in a pocket, he takes out a spray and sprays it upwards. Two policemen put their hands over their eyes as they scream, and then two others kick the man twice, once in his face and once in his chest.

Ngiyimpumputhe.

Angikwazi ukubona.

Mu bulale.

Mthathe.

Dear Mother, As-Salam-u-Alaikum Warahmatullah

I hope that you are well for I am well. But I am not so well for although this is the month where I must give up my earthly needs and in which I am purifying myself I am feeling great pain. I do not feel the pain because we must fast from sunrise to sunset, for I know that this is the time that I must be fully aware of Allah, may the Grace of Allah be upon you and my children, but because there has been a problem.

Eid Mubarak.

Unfortunately yesterday the police came to the shop, my shop and the one of my neighbour, my friend, the Nigerian man who is a Muslim. They confiscated many of the goods that we were selling and took them away. I do not know where they took them to. My friend, he was hurt badly, now he is in hospital. I think he might die. I am fine. But I know, and even more now in this time of Ramadan, that I must take care of him as he is my African brother. Allah, his Grace is upon us, requires this of me.

Regrettably I am unable to send you the money that I promised to send to you. Do not ask father to go to the Western Union for it will not be there. I hope Allah, Glory to Him, is able to forgive me for not sending this money, but I am unable to. I also hope that Allah, the Grace of Allah be upon them, can forgive these policemen who took our goods and who hurt my friend very badly.

Go in peace and do not worry about me.

In five days there is the crescent moon and we will celebrate with many fine sweets. Merriam is preparing for the festivity and I read the Koran daily to the children.

Your son Rashid

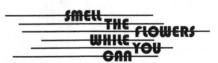

**Buildings are human.
They are places of secrets
and random happenings.
They are not there just
for the function that
they fulfil.**

*Buildings create an illusion, which
is itself an illusion, a new illusion.*
*This building is
my home.*

Just Some Stories of some unnamed Art Deco buildings

Building 1: Two grey Go-Away Birds sit above the concrete vertical protruding pilasters in the centre of the building. Another Go-Away Bird, it seems to be smaller than the other two, sits on one of two circular balconies. There is a flash, lightning, it lights up, just for a second, the grey streets and sunders the grey clouds. Then it is gone. After ten heartbeats there is a bang, a crack, but it is not a gunshot, nor is it a car that smashes into another car, nor is it the crashing of a glass bottle against the wall of the now empty passage way of the building. It is thunder, crack, and then there is a yawning growl. The birds' feathers are wet for it is raining, hard, but this rain will stop shortly for this is a Highveld storm, it is not designed to last. The birds are aware of this and sit stoically, soon the rain will be over and they may, should they choose, fly away. The smaller of the birds that sits on a protruding parapet, possibly she is the mother bird, flies down to the circular lip where she joins the two Go-Away Birds. It is safer here. It will not, she believes, be struck by a lightning bolt, and, if she sits on the left side of it she will not get as wet as she was when she sat on the right. The wind is blowing to the north and so, if she sits in the lee of the wall, she will be protected. The three birds remain on the building until the storm passes, twenty minutes, then they fly away. As they do so, beneath the building, people emerge from their shelters and ooze onto the streets. And then they continue with whatever it was they were doing before the storm began.

Building 2: On a balcony underneath two pairs of trousers, both are green, or at least a faded green, an olive green, three red and white T-shirts, numerous underpants, at least seven, and a light blue dress, is a birds' nest. It is small, the home of a sparrow, one of two that flies from the top of the building down to the street and pecks at the left over pieces of bread, or dried out pap, which lies there for it has not landed in the dustbin when it was thrown from a window. There are two dustbins, one on either side of the entrance of the building. The nest is made of untidy pieces of thin sticks, dried orange peel and leaves and black and white feathers. The nest is three quarters of the way up the wall, near one of the balcony walls, it is built on a small off-white marble ledge that protrudes from the yellowing concrete. On the marble ledges are glass bottles and other detritus.

The nest contains two white eggs that are speckled with green and reddish brown dots. These dots are not organised symmetrically, they are etched into the eggs haphazardly, as if a painter took a paint brush, dipped it into paint and flicked it across them. The nest and the eggs are covered in newspaper, but it is not fixed to the wall and so it flutters in the light breeze as if it is a feather, a feather that tells the world its news. The female sparrow, her beak is not as yellow as the beak of the male, flies down to the street. Then she flies up again and sits on the block-shaped horizontal entablature on which the name of the building is written. She makes a call to her mate who is close to the nest. He guards the eggs from poachers and pilferers - chirrup. He replies to say that all is safe in this bay for even though this is a cruel and savage place, it is lovely and has such tenderness.

Building 3: The stairs inside the building wind their way upwards. They are circular and have metal iron balustrades; they are worn smooth from the hands that have touched them, caressed them, held and grasped them. On the third floor, this is the top floor of the building, just below the flat roof, and about three meters from when the stairs end are the remnants of a meal, scattered bones, they could be chicken bones, are heaped in the southern corner of the floor. The bones hug the corner walls and form a patterned triangle, a wish bone. Next to the bones, there must be at least ten of them, is a mouse. The mouse has dark brown fur, three golden stripes run from her head down to a tail that is thick and fluffy. She does not run when she hears footsteps on the stairs. She has four whiskers on either side of her face; they shudder and twitch as if they are alive in themselves. She leans backwards and sits on her two back legs, then she takes a chicken bone between her front paws and begins to gnaw the fragments of meat that have been left on it, then just as quickly as she picks the bone up so she drops it. Then she runs along the wall, she follows it to the stairs, she jumps down the stairs, one step at a time, and on the second floor she stops. In front of her is an open doorway. At the entrance to the room she turns and seems to smile before running through the door and into the warm inside darkness. Once inside she again raises herself onto her back legs and begins to clean her whiskers, one at a time, then she

drops onto all four legs and runs across the dark parquet floor that is broken in places and outside an open door that leads onto a balcony. She sits in the sun outside. In the corner, on a decorative triangular tympanum, is a mouse nest, it is made from the offcuts of old clothing, purple silk underwear and green cotton shirts. In the nest are four baby mice, they have no brown fur and no golden stripes on them. They are blind and cannot run to the top of the building to read its name, which is raised and painted red. The mouse sits again on her back legs and watches the mice-lings, her children; she protects them from the disorder in the building, the disorder of the people that race up the stairs and onto the balconies seeking adventure. She sits quietly in her corner, a mouse that is not in the crowd, yet she is in the lives of others, the space of others, but as no-one knows that she is there, no-one can ever disapprove.

Building 4: The three black plastic flower bags are next to the entrance of the building. They stand upright for they are filled with heavy dark wet soil, it has been recently watered. The bags have been places half inside and half outside the building, at least half of each black plastic bag is on the white marble entrance hall floor, and while the water does not seep out of the bags, they are wet and so the marble is marked by eddying patterns. The rest of the bag is outside the doorway, it leans towards the pavement. A butterfly that has white wings edged in blue and purple alights next to one of the black bags. She uncurls her long orange and black tongue and sips the water, then, when her thirst is satiated, she curls her tongue back upwards so that it is neatly tucked in a spiral beneath her chin. The bags have been put here so that the plants that are inside them can feel the sun which, as it faces east, only shines in this space in the mornings. In the bags orange and yellow and pink gerbera daisies grow, and, as it is summer, they are in full flower. The bag on the left has the orange flowers in it and the bags on the right the yellow and the pink. The flowers are open to the sun; they lean forward so that they can hold firmly onto its rays for they know that it will soon disappear behind the building and be lost to them until the next day. The orange and pink and yellow gerberas match the former opulence of the building, now it is painted in brown, but once it was pink and orange and rust. Now the flowers in the black bags are the yellow sunrise and floral pattern that once was painted on the fluted concrete stucco above which are raised brown stars. At night, when there is no sun and it is dark for the street light that is at the

entrance of the building no longer has a bulb in it, the pink and orange and yellow gerbera reach for the stars, for although the stars on the building are now brown there is still light.

Building 5: Tied to a pole outside the entrance of the building is a dog. He has short brown and white hair. In a few patches on his stomach and one on his back there is no hair, here he is pink, balding, he has a skin disease. He is thin and is of no particular breed. The leash that holds him is made of a green fibrous plastic rope; it is frayed in parts but still it is able to hold him fast. The rope is long, long enough to allow him to run almost into the street, but not so long that he will be run over by the stream of cars that are moving at a medium speed, possibly forty or fifty kilometres an hour. The vehicles, at times, depending upon where he runs, have to swerve slightly so as to avoid crashing into him. He runs all the time, he is never stationary, into the road, back to the pavement, back into the road; he hears the drivers of the cars curse him and he hears their hooters blast, but he is not deterred, no sooner has he returned to the pavement than he runs out into the street again. Next to him sits a cat, an orange and white cat. He is not tied up and can freely walk in and out of the building, off the pavement and into the street, anywhere, whenever and wherever he wants to. And he does. Sometimes he emerges silkily from the entrance of the building onto the pavement to sit in the sun; here he licks himself clean, at other times he licks the face of the dog, lovingly, as if he is the dog's parent, as if he wants to take care of him. The cat moves slightly, his orange and white fur blends into the paint work of the building for it too is yellow, a mustard yellow. On the balcony of the second floor is a child's bicycle and a red and green dress, it may have been placed there to dry as it has been washed or it is just there, an enhancement. Now the orange and white cat sits on this balcony, he must have climbed up the inside stairs and walked into the flat, he sits in the sun on the red and green dress. It is probable that he could no longer tolerate looking at the dog and his death wish, it exasperated him, he cannot understand it, he cannot stand it, he needs some succour from this sight. After ten minutes he disappears into the flat, a while later he can be seen walking along a corbel on the top parapet, he is now on the flat roof. He does not stay here for long, it is too hot. Now the orange and white cat again emerges from the doorway, he looks at the dog that is still tied to the leash. Again the dog runs into the street. Then the cat, using his right paw, that on closer look is

black, the claws of which are not withdrawn but extended, plays with the knot that ties the rope to the pole. The knot comes free and as the dog runs into the road there is a scream. Several of the cars swerve, two of the cars that swerve crash into each other, and another car smashes into the side of a dustbin that is on the pavement and attached to the light pole. The force of the crash shakes the light pole and the bulb drops to the street, it shatters. The dustbin flies off the pavement and rolls into the road where another car veers off the road to avoid it. The dog lies still; he does not get up from the road and run to the pavement. The orange and white cat sits in the sun. He seems to say 'I'm not crazy, my reality is just different to yours, I am the Cheshire Cat', and then he gets up and steps into the entrance of the building. And so he is here and now he is not.

Building 6: The name of the building and a date, 1929, are written underneath the roof. The letters that make up the name are circular and curved. Underneath, at street level, are painted pictures of people in colourful hats and jackets and dresses and shirts. If you look quickly at them they dance, and if the eye lingers on them a while they still move, just more slowly. The wind, or an illusion? Above the figures are the words KWA-MAKOTI and in brackets t/a *Hattie's*. This is a general goods store, as it has always been.

Building 7: The air is cold and dry, only where the sun shines is it not cold. A lizard runs from under a loose pavement stone. He lifts his head, tosses his chin, and looks up, his tail swirls from side to side, no-one notices him even though, on this street, in all these streets, he is well worth looking at. Dry leaves from the few plane trees that remain in the town, there are four of them here, two are in front of the building on the opposite side of the road and two are to the left of the entrance to the building, this is the south side, blow and crack, eddy and spin. Each leaf has three pointed edges, the tip on some of them curls downwards, on others it is straight, and on the sides of all the leaves are two triangular pieces. Several of the leaves have been broken and so what remain of them are only small brown crumbs. The building is narrow, it has four floors. The name of the building is written at the top. The leaves swirl in the wind; they move across the balconies, into the entrance hall, across the pilasters, and as they move so shapes of light play out and reflect from the broken windows and the left over stained glass. This is a concrete garden made by man where the red and yellow flowers are immortalised in the stained glass; and in the jungle of leaves on an uneven pavement where a lizard lives.

Building 8: The building is covered in concrete stucco. The main entrance to the building is open to the road. There is an empty chair on the pavement, a new and soft green and yellow cushion is on its seat. The chair is just outside two wood and metal doors. This is a chair where the security guard sits, but he is not here now. The entrance doors are not closed, an iron security gate with curlicue lattices stretches across the door, but it is not locked. A silver padlock hangs from one of the spiralled cross bars, it is a large padlock, secure, it cannot be cut though with bolt cutters. The floor to the entrance is worn smooth, many feet have passed over it, walked across it over many years, at least eighty if not more, so that in some areas the pattern has been obliterated, and in others the whorls are very faint, almost non-existent, extinct. This is a building that is not looked at often, or even admired, for from the outside it is not imposing, it is only on the inside that magic lounges for dark reflections that move inside and outside the glass dance on red paint, the purple flowers of wisteria hang in violet buds on a wound-up trellis that stretches across a passageway. On the third floor, from one of the porthole-shaped windows a bird looks out. Then he jumps from this peek-a-boo window which has no glass in it and perches on the red railing that runs along the walkway. He cannot fly. He looks like a cock, a chicken; his feathers are shaded from red to gold, his cowl is red and cartilaginous, the orange feathers of his neck become yellow as they move down his back, then they become purple and then red, and, somewhere near his black and white tail, they are blue. He sits on the red balustrade and crows, cock a doodle doo. Is this a common cock or a regal Red Jungle Fowl from the deciduous forests in the foothills of the Himalayas; a local or a migrant? The whole of the inside area of the building is covered in geometric patterns; parallel straight lines, zigzags, chevrons, diamond-shaped lozenges and animal motifs. The Red Jungle Fowl is a figurative sculpture that stares and crows and will not be supper for he knows that he has been brought here from far away and that only a common chicken will be the evening meal. Chickens are predictable, but the Red Jungle Fowl has the jauntiness of design, a vitality of the never seen before. There is no meaning or depth to a chicken, yet this immigrant bird pecks and crows and so a counter architecture grows. Now is tomorrow, there never is life after nostalgia.

Acknowledgements

In writing this text, I am indebted to, amongst others: Andy Warhol, E E Cummings, Lawrence Ferlinghetti, Woodie Guthrie, Filippo Tomasso Marinetti, Raymond Patterson, Lou Reed, J. L. Borges, W H Auden, Paul Eluard, Lewis Carroll and David Wojnarowicz.

Thank you Nelisiwe Mofutsanyana and Sreddy Yen, who accompanied me on the many visits and adventures in Springs where we talked to people, took photographs, fell in love with drug dealers, bought fake goods and ate in local eateries. Without them I would never have gone there and had the experiences that I had.

Barbara Adair is a novelist and writer. *In Tangier we Killed the Blue Parrot* was shortlisted for the Sunday Times Fiction Award in 2004. Her novel *End* was shortlisted for Africa Regional Commonwealth Prize. She contributed to *Queer Africa* and *Queer Africa 2*, and her writing, particularly her travel writing, has been widely published in literary magazines and anthologies. Her novel *WILL, the Passenger Delaying Flight...* was published by Modjaji Books in 2020 to critical acclaim. She is currently working with the Wits Writing Centre at the University of the Witwatersrand. In 2022 she received a Ph.D. in Creative Writing from the University of Pretoria.

Printed in the United States
by Baker & Taylor Publisher Services